Right On Time

By

Lauren Stansberry

DH Books are published by
DH Publishing Company
PO Box 333
Indianapolis, IN 46250

ISBN: 978-1-7336502-5-0
Cover design: Christopher Wilson
Publisher: DH Publishing Company

DH Books

ACKNOWLEDGEMENT

I would like to thank my family for their support. My mother who I would bounce ideas off, even when she didn't know it. My sister (in-law) who was the first to read my work. And to my friend Montez, who pointed me to the right people.

Prologue

The pullover T-shirt that she wore quickly came over her head and thrown to the floor, and her bra followed. His hands caressed her mounds he loved so much. Then his head fell into her breasts and he sucked hard on one as he moved his hand over the other. His mouth was now on the other breast and his hands were on the move again. She moaned at the pleasure he was giving her with his tongue. He worked the zipper of her jeans. Soon he had pulled them down along with the matching thong she was wearing. She was nude while his clothes were still on. But she could say nothing because his lovemaking turned her mind to mush.

She felt his tongue move from her breasts he was lavishing and then to her stomach and lower. He played his tongue around and inside her belly button. She would have never thought her belly button would be one of her many pleasure points. He knew how much she liked it from the moans she was giving him. "You like that, huh, baby?"

Speaking for her was out of the question. All she could do was to shake her head yes. Juan showered kisses all over. Sonja knew where he was headed. When she felt his breath on the hot spot between her thighs, her hips arched up from the sheer thought of his tongue playing with her clitoris. It excited her and when his mouth finally came on her mound, she gasped and closed her eyes from the pleasure.

CHAPTER 1

"**I'm** sorry, Mathis. It's just not working out for us. This breakup has been on our heels for longer than we've both known."

Sonja had never seen Mathis like this before. He was speechless. He had always had something to say. But he was sitting there like a deer in headlights. One reason she was breaking up with him. She continued, "Come on Mathis, you will find someone that will love you a lot more than I thought I did. And I love you, but only like a friend, not the forever love that you want."

She got up, walked across his condo towards the door. Mathis was still sitting in the same place. She had to keep her head up as she walked out. If he saw one sign of weakness, he wouldn't believe her break up speech.

Sonja reached the door but didn't look back at him.

"Goodbye, Mathis. I hope you have an enjoyable life."

Mathis was still on the couch thinking about what Sonja, the love of his life, had just said to him.

She just walked out of my life like that. I thought we had something special. The ring box weighed heavier in his pocket now. *I wanted to propose to her tonight. She couldn't have meant what she said. After all these years, she must love me as I love her. I'm not giving up on her that quickly. She's just testing me to see what I will do. And I know what to do.*

When she made it to her car, it relieved her. But before she started it up, she took a few deep breaths and gave herself a pat on the back. She had finally done it. They had been dating for about a year and a half. The first year was blissful. If he had even hinted about marriage, she would have jumped at the chance. But soon after their first

1

anniversary, he showed his true self. He became insanely jealous over those she worked with. As a midwife, she dealt with pregnant women and the fathers of their babies. Although, there were quite a few times when she would go out and guys would hit on her, but she turned them all down. It was difficult to even have lunch or dinner with him. He kept thinking the waiter, host, or a random guy would hit on her. All she knew was it was time to get out of that relationship and she did. She had a smile on her face that could light up the entire world.

As she was on her way home her work cell phone rang. She had a feeling it was Lani Gray's husband, Shawn, calling to tell her it was time for their child to be born. She quickly answered the phone.

"Hello, Lani, I mean, Sonja, her contractions have started," Shawn said frantically.

"I am on my way there okay, just deep breaths for you and her. And I'll be there in a flash."

Then he hung up the phone. Usually, he was very polite, but under the circumstances, she wouldn't hold it against him. She zoomed to their house as fast as she could without breaking the law. But when she got to the front door, she was star struck. The most gorgeous man she'd ever laid eyes on was standing in the door frame. She knew what Shawn looked like, and this was not the father-to-be.

"Hi, are you Sonja Jacobs, the midwife?" The gorgeous man asked in the sexiest and deepest voice she had ever heard.

I finally found my voice, "Yes, that's me."

"Okay, they're upstairs in the bedroom, follow me."

Anytime, anyplace, any day," she thought to herself. "I have to get my head in the game. I have to deliver this baby and I need to focus. But his butt sure looks good going upstairs. Stop it and focus!" She reprimanded herself.

I could hear the screams of the 26-year-old woman as I

2

headed to the delivery room. I had brought some herbs I have used before, just in case the pain was too unbearable. Before I got to the door, it flew open and Shawn came out and sat me in front of his wife's opened legs. He looked as if he was hurting as much or more than his wife. They already had boiling water and towels set aside as I asked on the last visit. I put on my gloves and went to work.

"Ah, there's another contraction, and get this baby out of me, and I hate you for this Shawn, and Shawn please don't leave me," Lani said.

"I could never leave you," Shawn said in a loving and terrified voice. She could see the love that he had for his wife. And no matter how hard she strangled his hand, he never moved from his spot.

After seven hours of labor, I finally saw a head full of hair.

"I see the head." Every time she did this, it never ceases to amaze her. "Okay, Lani, one last big push when I tell you. Keep your breathing steady, PUSH!" And out came this beautiful baby boy.

"It's a baby boy." Lani and Shawn wanted the sex of the baby to be a surprise Shawn opted not to cut the umbilical cord, so I did.

After cleaning the baby boy off, I wrapped him in a cloth diaper that was laying aside the baby bath, then gently handed him to his mother. Shawn's eyes had tears in them as he held his wife and she held their newborn son. As I turned around, I hadn't noticed that the man who walked me in was still in the room. I was so focused on the birth that I hadn't even noticed anyone else in the room except Lani and Shawn. But there he was, sitting looking as sexy as sin.

"Can you take me to the restroom so I can clean myself up?" I asked him. I already had my duffel bag in my hand to change out of my scrubs I was wearing for the birth.

"Yeah, sure, it's right through here." He said, but

3

looking at the baby. I came out of the restroom smelling fresh. I wanted to give the new parents some time alone with their son.

"You have the advantage over me because you know my name and occupation."

"Oh, sorry, it's just that was amazing. But even so, my mother would have my behind if she knew I had forgotten my manners in the presence of a beautiful woman. My name is Juan Delgado, godfather to the little bundle of joy you just helped deliver." He said with pride in his voice.

"You sound very proud and you're welcome," Sonja said as they walked into the room. The newfound family was still in the same spot that they were in when she left.

"Have you guys decided on a name yet?"

"Yes," Shawn began, "his name will be Ellis Delgado Gray. Ellis was Lani's father's name who has passed and Delgado, which is Juan's last name. I forgot introductions. Juan this is"

"We have been introduced already when we stepped out and there are no reasons to apologize you were becoming a father." She said smiling just as hard as Juan.

Baby Ellis was one hour old and he was fed and now fast asleep, just like his mother. It was time for me to head out to go home.

"Congratulations, you have a handsome, bouncing baby boy. Well, I guess I should get out of here, but call me if you have questions or problems. You still have my numbers use to use when you need to." I was trying to inch my way towards the door and away from Juan.

"I have a suggestion," Shawn said with a smile on his face that said he was up to something. "Why don't you stay the night here since it's almost one in the morning? Juan is staying, and he lives just up the street. We have two spare bedrooms downstairs."

"That is such a nice offer, but I will to have to decline. I

4

make it a point to not spend the night over at a patient's home unless there is something wrong. Thank you, though."

"Well, you were officially off the clock when baby Ellis was born, and you've been here an extra hour. So, start looking at me and Lani as your friends. Besides, what kind of gentleman would you think Juan and me would be if we sent you out at one o'clock in the morning," He pulled every excuse out of the book on her.

She was tired and had a full day. "Okay, you got me. I keep extra overnight clothes in my car, just in case. I'll just get them."

"I'd better go with you just to be on the safe side," Juan said, surprising Sonja.

They were both silent as they descended the stairs and out to the car.

How could I have agreed to stay here when I know this man is staying under the same roof? I mean, we will not be in the same bedroom, but just walking next to him made me wobbly at my knees. What am I doing? Didn't I just get out of a relationship ten hours ago? But what does that have to do with anything? Nothing, I'm free to date whoever I please.

We got to my car, and I retrieved my overnight bag. Juan lightly pulled it out of my hands. Sonja gave him a what do you think you're doing look. Juan answered her unasked question.

"My mother taught me very well how to treat a woman." And gave her a smile with those lips she knew she wanted to sample.

He noticed her eyes settled on his lips and lingered there. So, he licked them real slow. She wished she was his tongue, or at least playing with it. He was saying we should go inside and get some sleep, which broke her from the trance she was in.

Sonja thought once she got into the bed, she would fall right to sleep, but she couldn't. Instead, a certain sexy man was on her mind. It only proved that Mathis was all wrong for her. Not once in their time together did her knees go weak just because he was around. Even though she had a full day, she was restless. It was odd. Usually, after such a long delivery, she would fall straight to sleep. But then again, you don't meet a man like Juan Delgado every day. She knew that Juan was keeping her from her good night's sleep because he was right across the hall from her. How could she be losing sleep over someone she just met? Besides, he was probably fast asleep in his room. And with that thought in her head, she finally drifted off to sleep.

Little did she know, Juan had been just as awake as she was. Even though he worried about the delivery and how Lani and baby Ellis would be okay, his eyes kept wandering back to Sonja. She did a splendid job of keeping everyone calm during the delivery. He liked how she worked. Juan knew he wanted to get to know her better outside of the delivery room. Sonja had a head full of naturally curly hair. She stood at about five feet eight inches and most of it was her beautiful legs. Even though a pair of scrubs bottoms covered her legs, he could tell they were defined. Her eyes were brown with a golden hue around the iris. It surprised him he got all that. He had only gotten a glimpse of her face when he opened the door for her. No other woman has ever attracted him like this before. She must be special. He wondered if she was married. He didn't see a ring on her finger, but how many people would wear a ring with latex gloves on and delivering a baby. I guess I can find out in the morning before she leaves.

Juan decided he would make breakfast for everyone. It was just going to be a way to congratulate the new parents.

6

CHAPTER 2

Juan got up early that same morning and heard the baby crying. It must have been time for another feeding. Baby Ellis had no mercy on his first-time parents. He woke everyone in the two-story house four times already. He heard Sonja's door open and close each time. He figured she was helping with the feedings, but he didn't know how because he knew Lani breastfed.

Juan rolled out of bed and headed for the shower. He didn't want to smell like a sweaty pig while he was making breakfast. What would Sonja think of him? After his nice cold shower and shave, he was on his way to his room wearing nothing, but a towel wrapped around his waist. He ran right into Sonja. While she was coming, he was going, and they collided.

They both fell into the carpeted hallway with Juan in between her legs. He had just got his hard-on under control, but now all that hard work flew right out of the window. He was as hard as a steel rod now. And he knew she felt it by the look on her face, so there was no reason for him to hide it. "This is turning into a wonderful morning," he said with a wink.

Sonja puts her hands on his chest but did not push him off of her. "You can get off me now."

"But I had a dream I was between your legs and here I am." Amazingly, his comment didn't insult her, instead it sent a shiver running down her spine. "Didn't you know you're still dreaming?" And she pinched him on his arm. He jumped right up and off her.

"Okay, sorry," he stated, "I hope you aren't leaving right away. I will make breakfast for everyone and serve it to the new parents. Would you like to help me?"

"Wait a minute, what just happened here?"

He put on the fakest smile. "I was just playing with you about the dream and all."

"Oh, really?"

"Would you have liked it if I was dreaming about you?" He heard the disappointment in her voice.

"Maybe," her smooth caramel skin turned a strawberry red, "besides, I felt how your erection came to life almost instantly."

"He likes you."

"Mmm, why don't we go out and see if it's more than that."

She stumped him. "Did you just ask me out on a date?"

As he looked at her innocent face, he continued, "Most ladies I know would wait for me to ask them out."

"Well, maybe you'll find that I am different from the other ladies that you have met. I don't believe in beating around the bush, especially with something I want."

"And I am happy to please you anyway I can." His eyes roamed up and down her body.

They exchanged numbers, and he promised to call her within the next couple of days to set the date.

"So what about breakfast? Are you in or out?"

"I can't, I have an appointment at eight. I am disappointed that I can't stay and talk more with you, but duty calls." She said sarcastically.

"Okay, then I will call you."

Sonja walked as quickly as she could into the bathroom and screamed in the towel that she had taken in with her. She couldn't figure out when she got so bold. She had never gone after anything like that in her life. What was it about Juan that brought this side of her out? The side she didn't even know.

                    *   *   *

The smell of the bacon awakened Shawn. He looked over at his wife. His eyes filled with love. Lani looked tired, but still so beautiful. She was a trooper. She had endured four feedings and three diaper changes, which Shawn handled, but Ellis wanted to wake everyone in the house. He couldn't love her more than he did right now. He carefully leaned over to kiss her on her lips so he wouldn't wake her up. He got up to see who had the house smelling so good. He knew it was Juan, but maybe Sonja was with him. As he got to the kitchen, he found Juan by himself. But he was wearing the biggest smile and there had to be a story behind it.

"What are you smiling so hard for?" Shawn asked, smiling with him.

"Good morning to you, too."

"Good morning. You didn't answer my question."

"Why are you all up in my business?" Shawn looked at him like he already knew the answer to the question. About three years ago, their positions were reversed. When Shawn and Lani met, she had to close an investigation that Shawn was the prime suspect. They had a whirlwind of a relationship from the beginning until the investigation was closed.

"Okay, okay. Sit down and I'll tell you what happened this morning."

Shawn sat down at the table, and Juan sat his breakfast in front of him. While Shawn ate Juan told him what happened earlier that morning.

"Well, you've been busy this morning. When are you going to call her?"

Juan smiled, "Later on tonight. Hopefully, she's not delivering a baby. But I am eager to get to know this Sonja Jacobs."

9

"I can tell by your big goofy smile."

Just then, they heard Lani's voice through the intercom, which startled both men. "You know, Shawn, you should have checked the intercom box before you started to talk like females. I heard the whole conversation. And can you please bring up my breakfast? Just thinking about Juan's cooking has my mouth-watering."

"Hey, has your mouth ever watered over my cooking?" Shawn asked, playing jealous while making her plate.

"No… my mouth waters for you in a whole different way." He could tell she was smiling.

"Wait a minute, didn't you just give birth early this morning?" Juan asked while checking his watch to make sure he was right.

"Yes," said Lani.

"What does that have to do with anything?" Shawn finished for his wife; obviously, they were thinking the same thing.

"Clearly, it means nothing to you two. I guess I should expect an announcement in a couple of months." They all started laughing.

Thirty minutes later, after Juan had gathered his belongings. He stood at the couple's door, "I am about to cut out and check in with the office and maybe do some work for a couple of hours. Call me if you need me. Bye"

"Bye." Lani and Shawn said, but while looking at baby Ellis. He amazed them.

CHAPTER 3

Shawn and Juan have known each other since college. They both proudly graduated from Howard University. They were college roommates. Their majors and minors were similar. The partnership just clicked. During their senior year at Howard, their dream became a reality. They hit their share of roadblocks, but they came out the winners at the end.

Today he had a meeting with the five top executive managers to hear how the progress was going on three of the company's high priority accounts. But all he could think about was Sonja. He needed to focus, but all he could see was her beautiful face. She was the best-looking woman he had ever had the pleasure of seeing. There's no denying that sparks were flying when they were near each other. I guess Shawn even felt it or he wouldn't have asked her to spend the night.

"And as you can see, Mr. Delgado, we are doing very well on the structure and we are ahead of schedule by about a week and a half."

"Thank you, Mr. Williams," I conclude the meeting.

"I am incredibly pleased that all the sites are doing an exceptional job and in a timely manner. I believe this concludes our meeting. I will send your congrats over to Shawn and Lani. And I will see you in two weeks. Thank you, gentlemen, for those precise reports."

Now that the meeting was over, he had some free time to call Sonja and set a date.

It was already one o'clock in the afternoon and he was eager to speak more with her. He passed by his assistant and asked for his messages, and he had none. "Make sure I am not disturbed for the next hour."

11

"Okay, boss." She said not looking up from her computer.

He continued into his office. So now all he had to do was make that call and set up a date with Sonja, and his day would be great. As he pressed the last number to her cell number. He got nervous. It was like everything around him disappeared when he heard her voice. It was sweet, kind, and he loved it. Her voice made him feel like he was floating on cloud nine.

"Hello… hello, is anyone there?"

He was so memorized by her voice he forgot to speak.

"Sonja, this is Juan. I guess I forgot what your voice sounded like because you had me speechless." That was a good line, he thought.

"Well, that was an excellent line." He could tell she was smiling at that.

"It's only a line when it's not true."

I was speechless.

"I was on cloud nine just listening to your voice, but I called to see if you're free for tomorrow night?"

"Thank you for the compliment and I am happy you called. I wasn't expecting a call from you until, like, Thursday."

"Why would I wait so long to hear your lovely voice?"

"Right, I am very much free tomorrow night and would be happy to accompany you out for the evening." He wondered why it was so hard for her to believe that her voice was as beautiful as she was.

"What are you planning for us?"

"Oh, something lite, you know, maybe dinner and maybe dancing." It would be hard to get reservations on a Thursday. He must figure something out because sitting on a waiting list was not ideal.

"I haven't gone dancing in ages, but I'm sure I can manage as long as you're leading me." He made a mental note dancing was definitely a must.

"What kind of dancing do you do?"

"I mostly do Salsa and Bachata add a little twerking to it. Do you know of those dances?"

"Ironically, I know them both extremely well. You would never hear me complain about you twerking on me. I will have to show you my moves." Drawing out the word moves which had her mind going haywire.

As they said their goodbyes, with promises to see each on Friday night.

Friday couldn't have come soon enough. They had talked more last night and agreed that he would pick her up at her house. He knew he was on cloud nine now, and there was no doubt about it. He knew it was all Sonja's fault, but he was so happy even those at work were excited for him. Their upcoming date was all he talked about. Juan wore a silly grin the entire day at work. He knew that just from being in her presence, his day would end on a wonderful note.

For their date, he had a standard dinner date and dancing, but then he figured that that was too ordinary for a woman like Sonja. So, he had a special evening laid out on the beach, just the two of them.

It was finally the end of the workday and all he had to do was go home, shower and change.

*   *   *

Sonja heard her doorbell ring, and she rushed to the door thinking it was Juan. He was to pick her up in about five minutes, but to her surprise, it was her two older brothers Tyrell and Zion.

"What's up little sister," Tyrell said.

13

"What are you guys doing here?" This was just great for her first date with Juan, and she had two unwanted bodyguards. This was not a good look.

"We heard about your break-up with Mathis, so we figured we stop by and see how you were doing," Z said, heading for her kitchen.

Unbelievable. They figured I would have nothing to do tonight, just because she had broken up with Mathis earlier in the week.

Sonja decided it was time to have a little fun with her brothers, at least until Juan got here.

"Thanks, guys. I can always count on you two," she said with a fake shy and sad smile.

Ty gave her a hug for comfort. "Why are you so dressed up?" Ty had noticed her attire first.

"Well, Ty, I just felt like being beautiful even though I wasn't going out tonight." *Did I have it that bad for Mathis that I would feel this bad for breaking up with him?*

"You're always beautiful." Z said on his way from the kitchen, with refreshments in hand, to her living room in front of her wall-mounted flat screen.

"Thank You, guys."

Just then the doorbell rang. A slow smile crept on her face. *Just when the fun was beginning, she thought.*

"Were you expecting someone?" Ty asked, and Z was peeking around the couch to see what was going on.

"Yes, I was," she went to the door to answer it. Ty and Z were now right behind her. She just knew it was Juan this time.

"Hello, Juan, come on in. Were my directions good enough for you to follow?"

He stepped into the house, "Yes, your directions were perfect." He leaned over and kissed her on the cheek. He didn't even notice the two men scolding at him from behind Sonja. Everything she wore, from scrubs to the beautiful

14

little black dress she wore now, looked good on her. This dress clung to her in all the right spots and outlined her slight hourglass shape perfectly.

"I should have told you this when we talked last night, but I planned to take you out on the beach and have a relaxing dinner."

"So, I should probably change."

"Yes, unless you want to get that unbelievably beautiful dress messy. And you look good in that dress." It was like they were in their own little world. They stared into each other's eyes for so long, that Ty and Z both cleared their throats as if to distract them. After a minute, Sonja remembered that they were still there and waiting for introductions.

"Oh, these guys behind me are my brothers, Tyrell and Zion. Ty and Z, this is Juan Delgado, my date for the evening."

They looked at her as if it hurt them. "I thought you said you didn't have a date tonight?" Ty asked, looking up at Juan now.

"No, you assumed I would be lonely because I broke up with Mathis. But that doesn't mean that I will be moping around. As you can see, I have moved on." She turned back towards Juan and grabbed his hand to lead him into the living room. "You can sit on the couch and wait for me to change."

She walked back to the end of the hallway and into her bedroom. Ty and Z had followed them into the living room. Tyrell, who Sonja had introduced first, so he assumed he was the oldest, had just stared at him with a look that said he didn't like him at all. *Standard big brother stuff*, Juan thought.

"What's your business with our sister?" He asked.

"As you just heard Sonja and me are going on our first date tonight," Juan answered in a calm voice that said their

15

protective role didn't scare him.

"Yeah, we got that. When did you two have the time to meet?"

"It was at the beginning of the week. It was that same Monday she delivered my godson. Sounds like it was busy for her." He had a younger sister, but this was a little over the top. Sonja was a grown woman of 30, at least his sister was younger, and pregnant with no man in her life. "I understand that you guys want to protect your sister. I have a younger sister too, and she's pregnant. But let me assure you that Sonja's in excellent hands."

"Why should we believe you?" Zion finally spoke up.

"All you can do is take my word that I will treat her the same way I would want someone to treat my sister."

"Okay," like he needed their permission to go out with Sonja. "But if something happens to her, you will answer to us," Zion said.

"Agreed," Juan knew how he would treat her. Just then Sonja walked back into the living room. She was wearing a khaki skirt and two tank tops that fit around her mounds attractively. Even in something so simple, she looked breathtaking.

"I hope my brothers didn't interrogate you with crazy questions or make you listen to my boring past."

"No, none of that, we just had to come to an understanding, isn't that right guys?" Juan asked her brothers.

"Yeah, Sonja, we just wanted to make sure you would be okay with this guy," Zion said, but even Sonja could tell that Ty still wasn't convinced.

Juan looked into Sonja's eyes, not caring that her brothers were watching, and placed an arm around her waist protectively. "Are you ready?"

"Yes, I'm ready for the evening to begin. You two can leave when we do, which is now. Let's go." Tyrell and

Zion, with his snacks, were out the door first while Juan waited for Sonja to turn out the lights and lock up the house.

In the car, Tyrell and Zion sat talking.

"Well, I like him. He's straightforward and respectable, even though we came on a little strong. He didn't act like he feared us. He can hold his own." Zion stated.

"Yeah, that is true. And he didn't let us size him up. Maybe we should take him out somewhere and see if he's what Sonja needs."

"Yeah, that's a great idea. Sonja would have our heads hanging above her fireplace if we gave him the third degree. If you feel you must 'size him up' more than you have, then you can do it the next time you see him with Sonja."

With Zion's plan in mind, Ty drove off, knowing from the looks that were being exchanged between Sonja and Juan they would see him again.

CHAPTER 4

"**So**, where are we going on this date?" Sonja asked when they were all settled in his car and was on their way to the beach.

"I am going for seclusion. Some alone time to get to know each other. And when I asked you out this week, I did not realize it was Wednesday, and I did not want us to be on a waiting list at any restaurant. But I couldn't wait until next week to take you out. And let me assure you, we won't get into anything too fast."

"And what makes you think I will get us into trouble?" At the red light, he turned his gaze toward her, "I know that I am attracted to you, and I think you feel it too. Things between us can go too far too fast if we're not careful…"

"And on the beach, we won't be interrupted by anyone."

"It keeps the focus on us. I like," Sonja finished for him.

"See, we're already thinking on the same page." He gave her a sexy smile that made her blood turn to hot lava. Twenty minutes later, they arrived at the beach and picked out a nice spot where they could watch the sunset. It was a beautiful setting for a first date. And he told her.

"It is a beautiful night and I have a very beautiful companion"

Sonja blushed, "Thank you."

"I whipped up some grilled fish, broccoli and cheese, which should be warm, and for dessert, chocolate-covered strawberries. I probably should have asked when we talked last, but are you allergic to any of this?"

"Thank God I'm not. It all sounds delicious."

"I hope you like it."

"And you cook too?" Sonja said.

"I'm glad I asked you out."

"I'm not going to live that down, am I?"

"I would like to see you try to live it down?" She said with a laugh.

At his nod, she turned around and looked at the houses behind them. "I wonder who lives in those houses. I bet it would be amazing to look out the window and see the beach every day. It would be a calming effect that would probably last the day."

"Hmm," was his only response because he knew who lived in that particular house behind him. He did. He didn't know why he didn't tell her yet, but maybe he would surprise her one day. Luckily, he had recently moved into the house and the neighbors didn't know his face yet.

As they sat eating, Juan brought up her former boyfriend. He figured he would get it out of the way.

"So, who is the guy you were with before me that your brothers wanted to comfort you through this time of 'loneliness'."

"His name was Mathis, we dated for about a year and a half. After a wonderful year had passed, he changed."

"He hit you?" Juan became instantly angered. *How dare another man put his hands on my woman?* His woman? He thought to himself. He just met her not a week ago, and she's already his woman.

"I wish he would." She said in a sarcastic voice. "No, it was something else. During that last half of the year, he became insanely jealous. He would follow me to my client's houses. I can't count the many times we spent arguing about him suspecting that I was cheating on him. After six months, I couldn't take it anymore. I broke up with him the same day I met you. And for the life of me, I don't know why I came on so strong towards you. I've never been so forward to ask a man out. You are my first, so to speak." She could tell by the look in his eyes he liked

19

that he created a first for her. He crept toward her. "I like that I gave you a first." He wrapped his arms around her waist. "I have never had a woman ask me out, which means it was a first for both of us. But if there are any other first that I can give you just let me know."

"Well… I've never been kissed on the beach before." The last words barely left her mouth as his lips came for her. He wanted to taste her lips from the start. They both felt a glut of electrical current when their lips touched. She had a unique taste, and he wanted to taste all of her. He would not taste all of her here on the beach. He groaned into the kiss and gently pushed her down. She was lying on the blanket. While his body was half on the blanket and half on her. They entwined their legs. He had to pull his lips away from hers. He had to know.

"Please tell me I'm not a rebound date?"
His question was like a cold bucket of water thrown on her entire body. She pushed him from her and looked at him like he was crazy. "Do you honestly think I would ask you out and still have feelings for my ex? I was the one to break up with him, not the other way. What kind of girl do you think I am?" She was hot, but not the way he wanted her.

"You just ruined a perfect moment for our first date. That was one hell of a kiss we just shared. But then you just had to ruin it with that foolish question."
Juan calmly restrained her at the waist and lifted her, so she was straddling him. "Hey," he said in a soft voice, "It has happened to me before, and even though we've just met, I like you. I would hate it if I were just a get back in the-game date. And by your reaction, I will say that's a solid no to my question." She nodded.

"Well, babe, that's all you had to say." He said with a laugh.
She could tell that he put it all on the table, then buried her face in the crack between his neck and shoulder. She began

20

placing little butterfly kisses there. His body came to life. Then his mouth found hers in a tongue thrashing kiss. She allowed his tongue to make love to her mouth. His hands scaled up and down her back, then cupping her lush bottom. She had to pull back to catch her breath. His breathing was also heavy and in need of a deep breath.

"Maybe it's time for us to go since we're on thin ice as it is." She said close to his mouth.

After he stole a brief kiss, "You're right, I'll take you home." They gathered the blanket and other things they had brought in silence. They were still on a high from the kisses they shared.

He drove them home while smooth jazz surrounded them inside the car. Juan reached over and gently pulled Sonja's hand and placed it on the gearshift and placed his hand on top of hers.

"You should concentrate on the road." She told him.

"You are a distraction because all I can think about is tasting your lips again. So, I did the next best thing. I just needed to touch you to make sure you're here and not just my imagination. Is that cool?"

"Yeah, that's fine by me." Wow, he is my kind of guy. She said to herself, blushing. His hand heated hers and he felt a shutter start in her hand and knew it ran through her entire body. He smiled, loving the fact that he affected her as she affected him.. He also wondered if she was this responsive with just their hands touching how she would be when they were in bed. Sonja already knew where his thoughts were at and she blushed.

He pulled up to her house. "Do you want to come in?"

"I don't know. We might get into trouble."

"The only thing that will happen is a goodnight kiss, maybe."

"Maybe?"

"Okay, we'll shake on it."

He took her hand and kissed her knuckles. "Deal," he got out of the car and came around to help her out. They got inside the door, and in the dark, they could see a broad pair of shoulders.

"Hey, love, I was wondering when you'd show up." It was Mathis, her ex-boyfriend, sitting comfortably on the couch.

CHAPTER 5

"**What** the hell are you doing in my house, and how the hell did you get in here?" Sonja asked. Juan saw how angry she was and stood behind her for support, but with his arm wrapped protectively around her waist.

Mathis gazed quickly went up to the guy behind her, seeing where his hand had landed made him angrier, "What are you doing with my woman?" He questioned Juan as if he still had a claim on Sonja, as if they were still together. Juan smoothly came around to her side with his hand still possessively around Sonja's waist. "I am not your concern, and neither is Sonja. This is not your house. I suggest you give her the key you've copied and leave."

"What did you just say? She is my woman and you're the one that doesn't belong here. You need to leave." Mathis was not a happy camper, but neither Juan nor Sonja knew why he was there.

"I invited him. You weren't, invited Mathis," Sonja said, speaking up. "Now give me my key, and I suggest you forget my address, my number, and my workplace. I thought I made myself clear when I broke up with you."

"Yeah, but I have something…" Mathis said holding up flowers.

"If you say another word, I'm calling the police. Now Get Out!" He stood there for a minute as if he thought she would change her mind. He could not believe this was the same woman that he dated for almost two years. When he still didn't move Sonja reached for her cell phone and went as far as dialing 911. Mathis finally strode over to them and gave her the key he took upon himself to make.

"You can have this one. This is not finished." Mathis said, looking Juan dead in his eyes as he exited her house.

23

After he slammed the door shut, Juan went to lock the door, then came up behind Sonja and wrapped his arms around her. She turned in the warmth of his embrace. He was happy she came willingly instead of pushing him away. She buried her face in his chest and cried. Juan didn't notice until he felt the wetness on his shirt.

He could barely hear her say she didn't give him a key to copy. "He must have stolen your keys and made copies of them."

She looked up at him with slightly swollen eyes, "You think he made more than one copy?"

"Yes, he said. 'you can have this one.' So, I can only assume that he made more. And I have to tell you I don't feel comfortable leaving you here all by yourself." Sonja was so wrapped up in his warmth she didn't notice he walked them over to the couch in the living room. But they were already there and sitting down.

"I've been here for three years, all by myself."

"Yeah, but you didn't have a psycho ex-boyfriend copying your front door key."

"He's not a psycho," she said with a snicker, "He's just not taking the breakup very well, that's all. And according to my brothers, it should have broken me."

"So that's why they were here when I came. I thought you'd invited them over to sum me up."

"I didn't need them to sum you up. I got a rather good sum up all by myself."

"Well, that's good to know," he said, giving her a smile that would have made her knees buckle if she wasn't sitting down, "I would feel better if we changed the lock tonight." She didn't have a back door just a front and what he assumed was a garage door.

"Are you trying to extend our date or are you genuinely concerned about my safety?" She smiled at him. Juan felt his heart do a flip-flop and smiled back at her.

"Both, but more so the second one than the first, you could be in danger with this man."

She got up from his lap. "Let's go get those locks. There is a Menards hardware store right around the corner."

*   *   *

Juan and Sonja were on their way back to her house with a brand-new lock. "How did you become a midwife?" They never covered the basics during their date. Once they started kissing, everything he wanted to ask, went right out the window.

"I have always loved babies. What turned me to becoming a midwife is when I was twelve- years old and my big cousin was pregnant. She promised me I could be in the delivery room when she gave birth. One night when I was spending the night at her house. We were getting the nursery ready for the baby. She had contractions, then her water broke. I was responsible for calling her husband, getting her night bag, and getting us both to the hospital. I had called the ambulance, but by the time they got there, they couldn't move her. The baby was ready to come. I got to witness the miracle of birth that night when his big head popped out and I was hooked ever since."

"How can you stomach it? I gagged at least five times when you delivered Ellis."

"Yes, having a strong stomach is a plus." They laughed.

"Besides, it'll be different when you're holding your wife's hand and your child comes out and starts crying knowing that you helped create life. What do you do for a living?"

"I own a construction company called S & J Construction. Shawn and I are the owners."

"So that's how you know Shawn and Lani."

"Yes, it's because of me they met, stayed together, and finally married. I was also the best man at their wedding. And now the proud godfather of their firstborn and all the other kids they have. I would never have thought I would own a company. I've always loved to build things, but it was Shawn, who put the idea of owning a company in my head. I owe him for the success we have today. And also, the beautiful woman I'm sitting next to."

"I was just over at Gray's house today. They are handling Ellis like pros. They already have him on a schedule."

"That is great news. I talked to Shawn yesterday, and he said Ellis isn't letting them get any sleep."

"That's common for any newborn baby. The first couple of weeks are usually like that."

As Juan was pulling up to her driveway, he said, "I know you don't need to be protected, but I feel the need to do that very thing. I will feel even better if you'd call your brothers and have one of them spend the night with you." She looked shocked that he would suggest her calling her brothers rather than him staying the night.

"I think it's sweet that you want me safe. It lets me know you care about me. And I agree I should have someone spend the night, but I don't want to call my overprotective brothers. Can you just stay with me? I have a guest room just waiting to be used."

He thought about it first while playing with her fingers. He loved the way they felt against his hand.

"Okay."

"Don't think nothing will happen either. I'm not that kind of girl." They laughed. "You can park your car on the other side of the garage." She opened the garage door with her remote control on her key ring. They came into the house through the kitchen. "Do you want anything to drink? I have wine, juice, or water?"

26

"Wine, please." He turned and saw the radio on the counter. "Do you mind some music?"

"No," she answered. "Go ahead, anything you choose is all right with me." Whatever station she had it on before was already playing one of his newest favorite songs by Montez Lafayette 'Cure (Break It Down)' was playing and he stuck with it. He came up behind Sonja and wrapped his arms around her stomach and swayed to the beat. He sandwiched her between his solid, hard body and the counter. She didn't finish pouring the wine, but turned in his arms and wrapped her hands around his neck.

They stayed like that, dancing in her kitchen through a couple more songs. "I guess we got to dance on this date after all." He said close to her ear and sent a shiver down her spine.

"Yeah, we did." Sonja took a step back. "Let me show you where the guest room is." She said smiling from ear to ear. She knew any longer wrapped in his arms and around his scent would have him in her bed tonight. He was being the perfect gentleman. She held onto his hand and intertwined their fingers. She could feel his thumb rubbing on her hand.

They got up to the bedrooms. Juan had no idea how he got up the stairs. It was torture watching her walk from behind. She was so beautiful. He wanted to run his hands up and down her body. Sonja broke his train of thought that was about to get him into trouble. "Here's your room and there's a bathroom through the closet. So we don't run into each other like last time." She giggled. "And my room is right across the hall."

"Do I still get a goodnight kiss?" Before she could get an answer out, his mouth was descending on hers. He wanted this kiss to be gentle, but her lips were so soft. The taste of her was so intoxicating. When she parted her lips to give his tongue access, he couldn't help himself. She felt him

27

deepen the kiss, and she wrapped her hands around the back of his head to push him closer while his hands were at his waist, pushing her hips to his.

He pulled back from her lips. She moaned a protest.

"You will to have to push away from me and go into your bedroom before we get ourselves in trouble," Juan said.

"What if I don't want you to stop? I don't mind a little trouble."

"You have to want me to stop because this is our first date."

She looked into his eyes and saw his desire there and also something else, but she couldn't put her finger on it. She saw his eyes drift back to her now swollen lips and said good night. He let her go into her room, knowing how much he wanted to follow her and make love to her.

Instead, Juan did the gentleman thing and went into the guest bedroom right across the hall. *It was so close, yet so far away.*

*   *   *

Juan couldn't get to sleep. He knew it had nothing to do with his surroundings. He could sleep anywhere. He was the main one that did most of the traveling in the company, and they knew him for sleeping in weird places. He knew the reason for his sleepless night was because he was in Sonja's house. Knowing that she was right across the hall was also nerve-wracking. Juan also knew if he was at home, he wouldn't be able to get Sonja out of his mind enough to get a good night's sleep. He turned to the other side to see if it was more comfortable than the position he was in earlier. He had tried. The he heard a soft knock on his door.

"Come in," He said, knowing it could only be Sonja.

Sonja peeked her head in, "I couldn't sleep. I came to see if you were up and wanted to talk some more."

"Okay, let's talk," Juan said with an enormous smile on his face.

They talked for such a long time, talking about the future they wanted, goals in life, hobbies, and a host of other things. After a while, they had finished talking and was laying comfortably beside each other. She fell asleep in his arms. Even though he was tempted to keep her in this bed with him. He knew it wouldn't be right. His mother would have a fit if she ever knew. Juan gently swept her up in his arms and took her into her bedroom, pulled the covers back, placed her on the bed, and tucked her in. She looked so peaceful he couldn't help but to place a kiss on her forehead, then quietly left the room. When he made it to his bed he finally drifted off to sleep.

CHAPTER 6

Thank God it's Saturday. Sonja thought as she lay in her bed. She remembered her and Juan talking for the better part of the night, then falling asleep in his arms. *He must have brought me to my room once I fell asleep with him.* Juan was the perfect gentleman. She couldn't have asked for better. She wondered what Juan thought of her. She couldn't believe how attracted she was to him. She just met him Monday, and he's already sleeping over her house. *"What am I thinking? At least he's not in my bed... yet. I just never thought I could be so bold with...."* She thought to herself.

Someone was knocking at her door, it was Juan. She ran to the full-length mirror to check her appearance.

"Just a minute," she said. She flew to the door and opened it a little so only her face was showing.

"I'm sorry to wake you up so early," he said, looking as gorgeous as he did last night, "but your brothers are at your front door and I didn't get it because they don't know that I'm here or what happened last night. Not that I'm afraid of them, but I am a guest in your home." He was rambling. This means two of one thing he feared my brothers, and that wouldn't be a first or he was nervous about what would happen between them this morning.

"Okay, let me put some other clothes on and I'll be out to answer the door with you." She said as she was closing the door. Juan nodded his head and leaned against the wall. Sonja was out in a flash wearing a terrycloth bathrobe, and even though Juan didn't think it was possible, she looked even more beautiful every time he saw her.

"Okay, we will tell my brothers..." He interrupted her when Juan settled his mouth over hers in a gentle morning

30

kiss. Even though the kiss was gentle and too quick for her, she forgot what she would say when he had released her mouth. "What was that for?"

"It's the proper way for a man to greet the most beautiful woman in the world, at least it is for me." He said smoothly, knowing he was racking up major brownie points in her book.

"Well, I can get used to that. Do you do this to all the ladies you spend the night with?"

"I don't make it a habit spending the night at a woman's house. This is my special treatment, and it's just for you. What were you saying before our good morning greeting?" He asked as they went down the stairs.

She had to think for a minute. His kiss frazzled her brain.

"Oh yeah, we'll tell them what happened with Mathis and why you spent the night after that, we'll just wing it."

"Okay."

Her brothers had a key to her house once upon a time, but when they both abused that right, she took them away. When she finally opened the door for her brothers. She had seen the smiles disappear on their faces. Juan was standing right behind protectively. They glared at her, then at him. She could tell by the glares that overprotective brother's card was about to be pulled out of its hiding place.

"Finally," they both spoke simultaneously. "What the hell is he doing here, Sonja?" They both yelled at her. Sonja would have laughed because they always said the same things. She would call them super twins, even though they are not twins at all. But she figured it was too serious of a situation for them.

"Hey, y'all, don't yell at her," Juan said before she said something, which she was happy to let him take over.

I can pull the protective card too, Juan thought. "If you guys will come in, we will explain what happen last night when we got back from our date, okay."

Zion was about to speak, but Ty beat him to the punch.

"This is our little sister's home, not yours. You have no right to invite us into her house."

"Last I checked Sonja was a grown woman and she can do as she pleases. And she doesn't have to tell you anything about what happened."

Zion's face looked as if he was thinking hard about something with his eyebrows frowning. "Ty, let's hear them out, then if we have to punch his face in. I mean come on if he did something wrong to Sonja, he wouldn't be standing there with her."

Thankful that her younger brother saw the logic before jumping down Juan's throat. At least she taught him something.

Ty then jumped on Zion, "We don't know him and that's our little sister. We've been protecting her since she was born."

"Well then, let me relieve you of your duties." Juan said, looking at her dead in her eyes, "She's mine now," turning to her brothers, "And what's mine I protect."

Ty and Juan stared at each other and Ty nodded his head as if saying it was okay for him to protect her. "Can we all just sit in the living room and discuss this?"

"Yeah, we can do that little sis." She let them go past her and Juan but pulled his hand back to ask him, "Did you mean that?"

"Every word," he bent down, knowing her brothers were watching, and gave her a peck on her mouth, "Let's go tell them what's going on."

She took a deep breath, "Okay."

"It's my pleasure, baby."

After they ate breakfast with her brothers, they excused themselves to go get cleaned and changed for the day. Then they could explain what happened with Mathis. She wore a

32

mint green jogging suit with an Afro puff sitting on top of her head. She looked so cute. Juan could picture a little girl that looked like her with the same hairstyle.

"I'll kill Mathis for doing this," Ty said.

"Thanks, we had you pegged all wrong. We thought…," Ty kept what he was thinking, deciding they already knew what he was thinking when he saw he was still there that morning, "Never mind what we thought."

"Yeah, thanks for taking care of our baby sister." Z finally spoke up.

Juan guessed he had finally got the approval of her brothers.

"The pleasure was and still is mine," Juan said, looking at Sonja and seeing her blush the color of a rose, while he shook hands with each of her brothers. He loved to see her blush.

How could I be falling for someone so fast? It's only been a week. His mom always said love knew no time.

"You can't kill him, Ty, and then I would have to visit my oldest brother in jail," Sonja said. "We'll just have to come up with a solution." Juan's and Sonja's eyes connected over her brother's heads.

And Juan knew her mind was working. If she was thinking about going to a hotel, she was mistaken. "Why doesn't she just stay at my place for a while? I live closer to Shawn and Lani's house, and I could monitor her most of the time." Juan said without breaking eye contact with Sonja. He was more asking her permission than her brothers, even though they believed they had a say in her life.

"Is all this necessary?" She asked him with a sigh.

"Why are you defending him, Sonja?" Her name flowed right off his lips, so sweet. "If I hadn't been here, what would he have done?" Juan finally came to her and wrapped her in his embrace, not caring her brothers were still there. "I know we just had our first date, but my feelings for you are strong, very strong. And to lose you when I have finally found you would break my heart." He told her, looking into her eyes. She knew he was telling the truth.

"Well, when you put it like that." She said with a smile. "But only for two weeks and if nothing happens, then I'm coming back home, deal?"

"Deal," Juan said, giving her a kiss that he only meant to be light, but the feel of her lips under his made him forget everything else, forgetting about her brothers being there and the problems were upon them. Sonja was just as caught up in the kiss, but when she heard someone clear their throat, she pulled back. But Juan wasn't finished with her lips yet and brought her head back into his.

"Thank God y'all didn't deepen that kiss," Z said sarcastically. This time when Sonja pulled back, Juan let her go but didn't let her leave his embrace.

"Sorry, guys. It slipped my mind that you were here. You know how it is when you're wrapped up with the woman you..." Juan halted and lost his thoughts. *Was I about to say, love?*

Sonja had got out of his embrace and went to the window to look outside. *Was he going to say, love? Do I love him?* She asked herself. Maybe who knows?

Ty and Zion looked at each other, knowing what the next word he would say. "Yeah, we know, but keep it lite in front of us, please. Well, baby sister, we see you're in good hands, we out." Zion said, heading to the door and Ty right on his heels.

"Bye sis. Take care of her man."

"I will," Juan said with a hand tightly around her waist. Sonja had to leave his embrace to go shut and lock the door.

She leaned against the door, knowing what she was about to do. She pushed off the door. She couldn't wait any

34

longer. The kiss they shared was nowhere near enough for her. He saw her running across the short distance and caught her in his arms. As she was going to her tiptoes, he leaned forward to meet her lips. Their mouths touched, and hers parted to grant him entry. Their tongues tangled with each other. She sucked his tongue. He was massaging her up and down her back and down to the curve of her lush bottom. She moaned against his mouth and he turned and pushed her against the wall. Her legs found their way around his waist. When they finally came up for air, they were both gasping. Juan could only let one word come out of his mouth. "Wow!"

"I'm sorry, I didn't mean to ravish you like that, but my brothers were here for way too long, and that last kiss was nothing. I wanted more of you."

"Anytime you want to ravish me, it will be my pleasure and yours." He had that wicked, sexy smile on his lips.

"What do you have planned for today?" He asked with her still pinned up against the wall.

"First, I have to get off this wall." She said blushing. He kissed her cheek where she was blushing, stepped back and they sat down on the couch with her in his lap. "Thank you, the only other thing I have to do is go check on Lani and Ellis, but that's not until about two in the afternoon. Why do you ask?"

"My sister is pregnant. I have to get some things for the baby. I was wondering if you would like to come with me then we could come back here, get your clothes for the next two weeks and then head over to Lani's house."

"That sounds like a plan to me. I'm ready if you are." After just one more kiss, they got up and left to go to the mall.

CHAPTER 7

In the mall, they looked at just about everything they had for babies, from baby baths to car seats, and everything in between.

"Why don't you give her a basket full of bottles, baby clothes, and other baby things that way she can have at least one of each?" Sonja said as they continued to look around.

"She already has enough clothes for the baby. I think I might get her this baby swing. My little niece would love that."

"She's having a girl! How precious! Tell me about your sister."

"Carolina is my younger sister. Our parents died when she was about four years old and I was ten years old. I don't even think she remembers them. We were put into the system after their car crash. We were soon adopted by the most loving couple. Mom and Dad only wanted one child at first, they were only going to take Carolina, but they saw I was not letting my little sister out of my sight, they adopted us both.

Carolina was seeing this guy and they dated for a while I believe, I never met him. She said I was way too overprotective of her and that she wanted to live. He got her pregnant and ran off with his ex-girlfriend without a backward glance. I don't think he knows about the baby. Now she is due in a month and the father is nowhere in sight. If God forbid, Carolina was unable to care for her daughter, I will assume responsibility."

"It happens to the best of women, men who want nothing but to try to tear them down to nothing."

"Yeah, she was pretty hurt by it. But she won't give me his name. She already knows what I would do to him.

Which color do you think I should get this swing in?"

"I like the soft yellow one."

"I was thinking the same thing." He said and kissed her forehead. He ordered it. The swing was to arrive at his house within the next week. "It's almost two, let's go pick up you some clothes and head over to Shawn's house." He took her hand in his as they walked out of the baby department.

*   *   *

"Hey there, stranger, I haven't seen you all weekend. Where have you been hiding?" Shawn asked Juan while giving him a big bear hug.

"I'll tell you about it," Juan said when they were hugging so that Sonja couldn't overhear that he was going to tell Shawn about last night. He stepped out of the way to let Sonja through.

"Sonja, how have you been? Things are going a little smoother with Ellis. We're learning more daily."

"I'm doing better." She blushed and slightly turned to Juan. And Shawn looked up with curious eyes between Juan and Sonja. "Where are Lani and Ellis? I need to do my check-up with them."

"They're in the nursery, down the hall and the doors on your right."

"Okay, Juan this will only take about an hour."

"Take your time, I'm in no rush," Juan said and gave her a peck on her cheek as she was about to leave.

"You know you're going to have to fill me in about what's going on between you two," Shawn said, as they were walking to the family room.

Juan told him everything that happened from the moment that he walked to Sonja's front door to the moment they walked through his.

"Man, you work fast. And by the look in your eyes, you're far from done." Shawn said grinning from ear to ear.

"Yeah, well, she's staying with me for at least two weeks. But if I had it my way, it might be longer than that."

"Oh man, do I hear wedding bells?"

"Maybe."

"Damn man, do you love her?"

"I think I do. I already claimed her as mine when we told her brothers. And I just have this feeling in my gut telling me that she belongs to me and I belong to her, and that we should be together. I think I would die if I were to lose her. I want her to be happy no matter what. When we were discussing all of this with her brothers and the word love almost slipped out of my mouth." He said with a smile, remembering how he had stopped what he was saying but knowing it was true. "Is that love?"

"It sure sounds like it to me."

*   *   *

"Welcome to my home," Juan said, as they walked through the front door with her bags in his hands.

"I just love your house." His living room was painted a salsa red, which she just loved. She often went to clubs on their Latin nights periodically.

My house is your house. For as long as you want it and me in your life, forever. He said to himself.

"I'll show you the guest room and then I will give you the grand tour." Sonja grabbed hold of his outstretched hand as they mounted the stairs and headed to the guest bedroom.

38

CHAPTER 8

As Juan came to a stop in front of the guest bedroom, she would occupy, he turned to her as she began, "I know it's been a long day but....,"

"You're probably tired," Juan interrupted her because he didn't want her to ask if they could make love tonight and have her regret it in the morning. "And want to get some rest. There's a bathroom in there so you should be good."
She placed her finger on his lips to stop him from finishing his departing words.

"What I was going to say, was I don't want to be alone tonight and if you could find the strength in you to hold me through the night?" He looked into her eyes and saw fear and hopefulness. *How can I refuse such a beautiful woman?* He couldn't.
He nodded, "The grand tour can wait. I would do anything for you. All you have to do is ask me." Then he lightly kissed her on the lips, took her hand in his, and went up to the master bedroom.
His master bedroom took up the whole third floor. His
Four-poster bed could fit at least two couples in it, with a gold comforter on top of it and matching pillows. He had a flat-screen on the opposite side of the wall. Not that she was materialistic, but she could tell business was good. He led her into the bathroom and told her she could change in there. His bathroom was just as spacious. The colors were gold and black. He had a stand-up shower with multiple shower heads and a bathtub that looked more like a Jacuzzi. She couldn't wait to try it out. She loved the colors on his floor.
Within a few minutes, she changed and was ready for bed.

"Who decorated your floor? It's really..." Juan, only in pajama bottoms, had stolen her breath.. His smooth chest rippled with muscles. She could tell he took excellent care of his body. She got a good look at his abs and the v that dipped below his waistline before he could pull a plain white T-shirt over the breathtaking view.

"My sister decorated my entire house." He said while blushing when she stopped mid-sentence because of his bare chest. "I gave her the colors for each room, and she took it from there. Come here, sweetheart." He softly said. The endearment sounded so right. She happily went into his arms. When she reached his embrace, he picked her up, turned down the covers, and placed her in the gigantic bed. After they settled into the soft bed, he braced his hands on the edge of the bed and lifted his body over hers and landed on his side of the bed, as if he was in the Olympics.

"Show off," Sonja said in a playful tone.

"Only for you, babe," he kissed her forehead and put his arms around her, spooning her back to his front. She fitted to him like she had been there before. She felt like she had finally come back to the place she knew, like home. "I want you to know that you are the only other woman that has been in this house other than my sister."

"You have a lot of great qualities Juan, but I have to ask why me?" She said in a sleepy voice. But before he could answer her, she had fallen asleep. *Will she believe me if I tell her I love her, even though we've known each other a little less than a week?* "It's because I love you."

It had been a long day for her. She needed her sleep, especially after they spent the last night talking. Yesterday when he saw her ex sitting on her couch as if he belonged there, he at first thought Sonja had changed her mind about them, then remembered that she asked him out. He knew in his heart that Mathis was uninvited. He wanted to beat him down right there into the ground.

All she needs to know is I will always protect her.. There was no question in his mind about if he was in love with

40

her. I love her. It just crept up on him out of nowhere. With that thought in his head, he fell into slumber with her.

*   *   *

Mathis sat outside Juan's home. *I can't believe she's sleeping at his house. No doubt he already has her in his bed, the little slut. They will both pay for the embarrassment they have caused me. I saw how the morning played out. They thought I had left, but I didn't. I saw them at the mall shopping for baby items. Whose baby were they shopping for? There's no way she's pregnant unless she had been cheating on me. But where would she find the time we were always together? And since I had her followed by a friend for about two months. Maybe it was for his baby's mama. It's fine, I could stay out here for months if I have to. I have to find a way back into her heart, all I have to do is get her alone.*

*   *   *

My hand gently kneaded her breasts. They were so soft, and her nipples looked like chocolate-covered raisins that he could devour in one sitting. I lifted my mouth from her neck and placed little kisses down her back. One hand started inching down her smooth belly, heading towards her feminine mound.... "Mmm, Juan, that feels so good."
Juan immediately came awake at the sound of Sonja's airless voice. He looked at the clock; it was midnight. He looked down to where his hands were. One was on her stomach inching downward and the other was cupping her breast. The picture he had created in his dream was a reality. He couldn't help but smile. *I guess I wasn't dreaming after all. Is my body that in tune with hers?*

41

He already knew the answer before he finished the question. *Yes.*

His manhood was at full attention of what he was doing and was ready to give pleasure to this woman, not just any woman but his woman, lying in his arms. While he was trying to get himself under control, she started grinding her ample butt into his throbbing manhood. Juan couldn't help but groan out his pleasure from it. He could feel the heat of her body through his thin silk pajama pants. "Sonja, I-I'm so sorry. I didn't even realize I had raised your nightie up your body and started caressing you." Juan tried to remove his hands from the positions they were in, but Sonja held them in place and started moving against him again and again.

"Oh baby, I'm only a man. If you don't stop..."

"I don't want you to stop." Those were the first words she said since he woke up.

"Are you sure?" Hoping she would say yes, because he was already at the end of his rope.

Instead of giving him a verbal answer, she turned in his arms, wrapped her hand around his neck, and gave him a deep tongue wrestling kiss. That was all the answer Juan needed. Still locked in the kiss Sonja put on him, her hands roamed under his T-shirt and followed through to his back where she raked her nails up and down.

Juan's hands were cupping her full behind and pushed the long nightie up the rest of her body until he reached where her breasts were. He found out she wore no underwear when she went to bed, which made his blood boil even more.

Sonja broke the kiss off and lifted his shirt over his head so she could have access to his chest. She pushed him onto his back. She straddled his legs and took her shirt off. Juan was as happy as a blue jay. "You are so beautiful." She placed kisses all over from his neck down to his chest and going

42

down even further. Before she reached his belly button, he pulled her up the length of his body, to his face, and turned them both over so she was beneath him, then gave her a deep kiss. "I couldn't take your hot mouth on me right now." Juan hopped out of the bed.

"Where are you going," worried that he was leaving her in this state.

"I need to get the condoms before I get lost in your sweetness, lovely." He said walking from his bathroom with a box of condoms. She was so far gone she hadn't even thought about protection.

While Juan was up, he stripped off his silk pajama bottoms. Even though she saw the bulge in his pants, it was nothing like looking at him nude. He was huge. He looked like a god standing before her. She couldn't take her eyes off of him, wondering if he was too big to fit. The head of his erection was angry and looked ready to burst. He opened the box of condoms and pulled one out and threw the box on the nightstand.

Sonja reached out to stroke his long erection. "Oh, baby, I can't take much more of that." She took the condom out of his hand. She tore it open with her teeth and rolled it slowly onto him. "That is the sexiest thing I have ever seen in my life." He grunted out as she finished putting on the condom. Before she could think of another way to torture him, he lifted her and placed her back on the bed. He could not help but caress her womanly core. As soon as she felt his fingertips, she moaned softly. He worked one finger, then two fingers into her womanly channel. She moved her hips into his fingers, wanting more to go in than what he was giving, just when it was getting good. He removed his fingers, and she moaned her protest. "You are so going to pay for that."

He smiled at her threat, knowing he would love her payback. She was laying on her back. Before she could say anything else, he parted her legs to make way for his body. His erection found her womanly core like a boat to a lighthouse. He inched slowly into her wet channel. Inch by inch he eased into her and when he was engulfed in her, he had to catch his breath. Never had it felt that good for him.

He hadn't known how long it had been for her, but she was tight. He took a few seconds for her body to adjust to his size. Then he slowly moved, in and out. Sonja met his thrust. His hands were under her, pushing her so he could get even deeper. Their moans and groans mingled in the air. As he felt her tighten around him, he knew she was close. He quickened his pace and put the force of his entire body into his thrusts. He could feel her getting wetter even through the latex separating them. She arched her back high off the bed as her first orgasm hit her like a tidal wave.

Sonja rolled them both over with her strength she didn't even know she had and moved on top of him. "You like to be on top, baby. Oh, baby." She knew that his release was right around the corner. She moved her hand around their bodies and stroked his tight sacks. She felt him come even through the condom and by the loud rumble he let out with his release. It triggered her second release. She swore she saw fireworks behind her eyelids as she collapsed on top of his heavily breathing chest.

Juan rolled them over on their side. He pulled out of her, went into the bathroom and cleaned himself off and brought the washcloth to her so he could clean her off too. After they were cleaned enough, he cuddled up beside her and they fell asleep in each other's arms.

CHAPTER 9

Who could call at this hour and right before he was about to get some more love from Sonja? He couldn't believe how much he loved her.

"Hello," he asked in an annoyed voice. "Yeah, are you sure?" Another pause, "Okay, I'm on my way."
He turned to Sonja with a smile. "Do you want to hang with me today? I promise to show you a good time." He said while planting small kisses on her neck.

"I wouldn't want to do anything else with my time. Where are we going?"

"To the hospital," he saw the face she gave him. He smiled even harder. "That was my sister's best friend, and she's in labor right now. So, we have to go right now." He moved away from the bed. "You want to grab a shower with me?"

"I thought you said you wanted to leave soon, like, now. If we go in there together, we'll take forever. Are you sure your sister won't mind me coming to the hospital while she's in labor?"

"No, she won't get mad or anything. She's cool, and I wanted you to meet her soon, anyway. And the shower is big enough for both of us to be inside and not touch each other. And I promise not to touch."

"I will go only if you promise not to start anything."

"I promise."
She pulled the covers back, got up, and walked into the bathroom. She was as comfortable in her skin as he was. Juan could do nothing but let his eyes follow her, and then he remembered that he would shower with her, so he followed. *Today will be a delighted day.* Sonja thought as she saw him following her.

Carolina, his sister, was having a hard time giving birth regularly. They took her to the operating room to do a C-section. Juan had no idea what was going on with his little sister, and he was freaking out. Sonja tried to hold him and tell him that everything will be fine. He just couldn't sit still, and she couldn't blame him. It was hard sitting and waiting for the doctor to tell you a loved one was okay or not. An hour later, the doctor came through the door.

"Mr. Delgado, I'm Dr. Kelly, Caroline's OBGYN. There were some problems with the birth. I have good and bad news." Sonja saw Juan's jaw tighten.

"You are the uncle of a newborn boy. He is six pounds, ten ounces, and is twenty-one and a half inches long. Congratulations." Juan was so happy the baby was safe.

"But" there was always a 'but' in the mix of things.

"Carolina is not doing so well. During labor, my nurse saw signs of her having a stroke and I knew we had to get the baby out as soon as possible. After the birth, she went into a coma." Both Juan and Sonja gasped out loud. "I'm very sorry, but there's nothing we can do until she comes out of the coma."

"Can we go see them, both of them?" Juan asked in a shaky voice. The doctor nodded and stated a nurse will be around to collect them.

"I know this will be a tough time for you, Juan. I don't have to go with you." Sonja said with sad eyes.

"You're right, but I don't want to go alone. Can you please come with me, please?"

I will be there for him. Just like he was there for me, "I will come. I just didn't want to intrude."

"You can never intrude into my life. I want you here by my side, always." He gave her a sad smile and held her hand tight.

46

"Yes." Sonja didn't know if it was because he was emotional about his sister, but his words warmed her heart.
The nurse came out for them to follow her to his sister's room. "We have already prepared both of them, if you'll follow me, please. Do you know what she will name the baby?"

"No, she told me she was having a girl. But she always said if she had a boy, she would name him after our biological father. Diego Miguel Delgado. Am I to sign the birth certificate, with her name?" He asked as they followed the nurse into the hall.

"Yes, that's fine." The nurse stopped in front of a hospital room.

"Your sister is in this room and I will have a nurse from the nursey bring down your nephew."

"Thank you, ma'am."

*   *   *

Carolina was so still. *This cannot be happening. She should celebrate and cuddling her newborn son. I can't lose her, she's the only biological family that I have. This is crazy.* "She would have loved you. She was so full of life and joy." The nurse came into the room with Diego.

"The birth certificate is ready for you to sign."

"Oh, he is a handsome little guy," Sonja said as she picked the baby up and handed him to Juan. Juan held the baby boy. It was as if he was holding himself. Diego looked just like him.

"Wow, he looks just like me when I was a baby." Sonja saw the man who loved his family. They made a beautiful picture, even though his sister was in a coma. Tears filled her eyes. She pulled out her phone to take a picture, knowing later in life it would be important to all three of them.

47

"I will go get some coffee from the lounge. Did you want some?" He shook his head no, and she left the room. He was such a beautiful person, inside and out. He would have a lot on his plate dealing with his sister and Diego. She wondered where it left them. Is she still going to be staying with him for the rest of the two weeks? She would ask him in a couple of days when the baby was to get discharged from the hospital. She returned to the room, as Juan was feeding the baby.

"I guess in a few days we'll have a roommate," he looked up at Sonja, "if you don't mind late-night crying."

"If you want me to find someplace else to stay for the next couple of weeks, it'll be no problem."

"Please, no, I would feel more comfortable with you with me. I have no idea how to care for a newborn. I don't even know how to change a diaper. The doctor said he is healthy and that he could go home tomorrow afternoon."
She went to his side, "I'll help you. Hey, look, he's asleep again. Did he open his eyes for you?"

"Yeah, they're a greenish-gold color. Just like mine when I was a baby." Sonja looked confused. His eyes were dark forest green, almost black. "But mine got darker when I grew up. His eyes will probably do the same."
They had spent the rest of the day up at the hospital together. It was a sad and happy day for Juan. On one hand, he had his sister who was in a coma after giving birth to a healthy baby boy, and he had Sonja, the newfound love of his life. He had never experienced with other women what he had with Sonja. She brought out a side of him he didn't know about until he met her. He didn't dare tell her how he felt, not just yet. He didn't want her to think because his sister was in a coma he was feeling lonely and his heart had mixed feelings.

CHAPTER 10

Later that night, at about eleven, Juan pulled into his driveway. He was reluctant to leave his sister alone in the hospital, just in case she woke up, but the nurse promised to call him if her condition changed. Both of them were beat, but they knew they had to get things ready for the baby. They got the crib and some other things from Carolina's two-bedroom apartment and brouhgt it to Juan's house. Tomorrow Juan would bring Diego there, to his uncle's home. While Sonja stayed at the house to make sure everything was in order. Hopefully, Carolina would come out of her coma because her son and brother would need her. She was glad she had not heard from Mathis in the last couple of days, not even a phone call. She figured that Juan had shaken him up pretty badly.

Juan had gathered up the baby crib, the car seat, all the baby clothes, diapers, baby bath items, bottles, all the baby milk formula, and anything else he thought they would need to care for Diego.

It was time to go get the baby. Sonja knew Juan would check in with his sister. He came home around five that evening. Sonja had dinner already waiting for him. "I made you some grilled chicken, macaroni and cheese, and green beans. I can't believe you're home," stunned that she said home and not your house, Juan just raised an eyebrow, "I mean…"

"I love that you consider this your home." He said with a wicked smile like he was up to something. "You never know what can go down." He gave her a kiss, wrapping his arm around her waist and the other arm holding the car seat. This kiss was just like all the other ones they had shared. The baby cried signifying that he was hungry or wet. They broke off the kiss and went into the living room. Sonja took him out and checked his diaper. It was dry. She heard a mumble, "Thank you" come from Juan.

"You know that in a few he will have a dirty diaper. And you will have to watch me clean it the first couple of times." She said with an amused smile of her own.

"I thought you liked me."

"You know I do, but you have to learn it for yourself. You have a plate of food in the microwave." She said as she went into the kitchen to prepare the baby's dinner, nice warm milk. Juan followed her holding the baby. "Use half a scope of the powdered milk per ounce of water. Then shake it up good and put it under hot water until it was warm but not scalding hot. Okay?" He nodded his head yes. "I can feed him while you're eating." She took Diego from him and went to his food.

Sonja sat at the table Indian style with Diego in her hand feeding him and talking to him. She would make a wonderful wife and mother. She was very nurturing. He would be so proud if she agreed to marry him. But he didn't want to scare her off with his words of love. They made a wonderful team, and they were handling Diego very well.

The timer on the microwave broke his train of thought and he got his plate and sat next to Sonja. They were lost in their thoughts, in comfortable silence.

Soon Diego was asleep, and Sonja walked him up to his room and lay him in his crib. She came back down the stairs and said, "Okay, we have at least two hours of playtime." Juan was sitting on the couch watching something on the television but wasn't paying attention when she entered the room.

"What will we do with all that time on our hands?" He said with that sexy wicked grin again.

"I have a few suggestions, but first we have to talk. I want to know if there are any changes with Carolina." She said as she leaned against the stair banister.

"Well, she's the same. She has always told me that if she was to go into a coma, then I should think about cutting life support off after a month. But how could she ask me to do that? How can I do that and explain that to her son what happened to her?"

"I know it's hard and I don't know what I would do in the situation. Your sister is a strong woman. She will pull through this and you all will be a happy family."

"Will you be in my family?"

"Do you want me to be?" She answered his question with a question; just to be sure, they agreed.
He got up from the couch, walked over to her, and wrapped his arms around her. He put one hand on her chin and lifted her head, so she was looking right into his deep forest green eyes.

"I do."
She blushed, "So I guess you sort of like me."

"That's where you're wrong." Her face dropped, but he held onto her chin, so she was still looking him in the eyes.

"I sort of love you."
Shock spread through her face, then joyfulness. Tears ran down her face. "I love you, too." That was all Juan needed to hear. He zeroed in on her mouth and took the kiss he had been waiting for. They were going for each other's clothes, but before Juan could fully cup her breast. She pushed him away and took off up the stairs.
A smile spread across his face, knowing exactly where she was headed. He followed her. He couldn't believe she felt the same way he did only after the week and a half that they spent together. When he got to the room she wasn't there, but he heard the shower going. He removed the rest of his clothes and stepped into the bathroom. She was in the

corner seat inside of the shower, looking at him as he entered the bathroom. He opened the shower door with his manhood sticking out from his body. "You know, after all these years I have never made love to the woman I love in this shower."

"I will be the only woman in this shower with you, got it?" She said as he entered the shower to join her and giving him a hard but playful stare.

"Yes, ma'am," they laughed. "Time is slipping away with every word we say. Let's get this party started." He said as he walked towards her and she grabbed a hold of him. "I assume you are healthy. And just in case you're wondering, I have had a checkup a month ago and got a clean bill of health." He nodded his head because he could not speak with her soft hand around his stiff member. She trusted him to tell her the truth. She let him walk towards her and when he got directly in front of her, she put her soft mouth on his extra sensitive tip and sucked. He had to brace himself by leaning his hands on the shower wall. She continued to suck at his tip, then allowed him to go deeper into her mouth. "Oh, my god, Sonja, your mouth is so hot." Her moan vibrated throughout his entire body. She wanted to devour him. She could tell that he was close. Not wanting his seed to spill into her mouth, he pulled back from her and went to the other side of the shower where he spilled out his seed and it went down the drain. "I am so going to get you for that."

As he started walking towards her, he heard the baby starting to cry. "That's the baby monitor. I guess you'll have to get me some other time." She hurried out of the shower and slipped into a plush bathrobe and headed out the door and to the nursery. After he cleaned himself, he grabbed the bath towel on the warmer and went into the bedroom to wait for her. *I don't need to be there for every diaper change.* As soon as the words were a thought in his

52

head, he heard Sonja through the baby monitor that he carried in the bathroom. "Hun, you need to be in here for this diaper change. And I know you can hear me because of the baby monitor." She said with amusement in her voice. He made his way downstairs and into the nursery.

He knew why she was laughing when he came into the room. The first time she showed him how to change a diaper, Diego had left a huge load in his diaper. The smell was horrible. He had gagged multiple times. And she thought it was hilarious. Now he would have to go through that same torture.

"He didn't leave you a big load like last time. He just peed, but with boys, look out for pee in the face."

He knew Sonja would get him because his attention was not on learning how to change a diaper, but it was on her and how caring she had been for stepping up to a responsibility that wasn't even hers to take care of. When Carolina comes out of her coma, he will do right by her and marry her. He could not think of life without her, and he didn't want to think about her not being there for him.

CHAPTER 11

"**Had** it been two weeks already?" Sonja asked herself. She had been staying with the baby while Juan went to work and went out to visit with Carolina. He would sometimes come back home and pick them up before he went to the hospital. Saying that Diego should be able to see his mother even in the state of being she was in. Diego was getting big; from the time they brought him home from the hospital. He had gained four more pounds from his birth weight. He had smiled. It had been a hassle, but we got him on a schedule. It was now regular for him to wake up twice a night instead of him waking every hour. Juan was a good learner with his nephew. She could see the love in his eyes every time he talked about Diego or held him. They had not discussed if she was staying at his house, or if she was going back home.

As they lay in bed, after the last nightly call from Diego, she brought up the subject.

"Juan you know, we never talked about what we would do beyond the two weeks that I agreed to stay here."

"I know," he sighed, "I was hoping you would forget about that and just live here with me."

"I didn't want you to think I was outstaying my visit."

"You call this a visit. You've stayed in my bed for the whole two weeks that you have been here. I would not mind if you moved in with me."

"You're not getting off that easy. I want to be married before I move in with someone."

"But there's a difference here because I'm someone you love."

"Are you saying you don't want to marry me?"

"It might come," he said with a smile, "soon." He had

already bought the ring to give to her. He was just waiting for the right moment. She smiled up at him and lightly kissed him on the lips.

"Now I have to be on the lookout." She reached for the drawer to look for the ring box.

"It's not in there. If you can find it, then I will get on bended knee right on the spot." He knew she would never find it because he hid it in a secret drawer in the closet. As he kissed her on her neck, the phone rang. "Who would call this late?"

"Maybe it's your ex wanting you back." She said that because they went out on their second date and ran into one of his ex-girlfriends. But she seemed nice enough and there were no hard feelings that she knew about and the breakup between them was mutual.

"Yeah, right," he said as he grabbed the phone. "She is. I will be there as soon as I can. Thank you, doctor," Sonja could tell it was good news concerning his sister. He jumped up out of the bed, "She came out of the coma and we have to get up there right away. I can get Diego together and ready to go see his mother." The smile on his face was so bright it made her smile.

*   *   *

They got ready and up to the hospital as fast as they could. They entered the room as the nurse was finishing up with checking her vitals.

"Carolina," he said her name in a breathless whisper. And Sonja had tears in her eyes from the overwhelmingly happy occasion. He hugged her and kissed her on her cheek. "There are some people here that you should meet. First here is your son, Diego Miguel Delgado, since you

55

only had girl names picked out, I had to choose. I named him after our biological father. And this lovely lady here is my newfound love, Sonja Jacobs."

"I had a boy? But they told me I was having a girl. He looks just like you. How can that be when he's my son? I have all girl clothes at home." She said playfully. Juan had finally put Diego in her arms. After two weeks, this reunion was long overdue. She looked so happy. As she was holding the baby, her monitor started beeping and her eyes rolled to the back of her head. Juan quickly scooped up Diego from her arms while Sonja ran out of the room to get a nurse or doctor.

"Can you please wait outside? We will do everything in our power to help her," the nurse said while pushing them out of the door.

An hour later a nurse came out and said they were taking her to get some surgery done. Juan was going out of his mind with worry. Thankfully, he had taken the time to make some bottles for Diego before they left the house. Another hour had passed, and a doctor had called them to give them the news of Carolina.

"Hello, I'm Dr. Ronald Kens; I was the surgeon who helped with Carolina. During labor Carolina's brain swelled and because of the coma, we could do nothing about it. Not without her being alert. She was gone for a minute, but we were able to bring her back. But she has slipped back into her coma."

Thankfully, a chair was behind Juan because his legs gave out on him. After seeing her awake and talking, he thought she would be all right. "Baby, I am so sorry." It was all she could say to comfort him. But she held on tight, not letting him go. His hands were covering his face. She could feel his pain, and in some odd way, she was in as much pain as he was. He took her arms from around him and stood, thanked the doctor for his help, and gathered up their belongings. The ride home was strained. Neither one of them spoke. Sonja didn't know what to say. She couldn't read his face and didn't know what he was thinking. Lost in his thoughts and she was straining to hear what he wanted to say. She could only imagine what kind of pain he was feeling over his sister, not knowing if she would come out of her coma. He thought the smoke had cleared and everything would be fine from here on out.

Once they got to the house, he opened the door for them and went straight to their bedroom. He didn't bother to ask about his nephew. He knew that she understood. She didn't fight him about it. She had taken care of Diego. He was soon asleep in his crib.

Sonja didn't want to disturb Juan in the bedroom. She stayed in the nursery and tried to get comfortable in the rocking chair. She had finally found a suitable position when she heard a sound in the kitchen, not thinking it was Juan but a burglar, she grabbed the nearest weapon she could find, which was the folded-up baby stroller. She waited at the door of the kitchen for the person to walk out and when he did; she swung the baby stroller like it was a baseball bat.

Juan's quick reflexes kicked in and he dunked. "Baby, what the hell are you doing?"

"I thought you were a burglar. You scared me half to death, making all that noise."

"I've been looking for you. I thought you left. But I still saw your clothes and figured you were somewhere in the house."

"Why would I leave when you still need me?"

"Where were you?"

"I was in the nursery trying to get comfortable in the rocking chair. I thought you wanted to be alone. I didn't want to disturb you. So, I stayed in there."

He pulled her into his arms. "I need you now. I can't sleep without you. You are my strength when I don't think I can carry on. I love you."

Before she could tell him how much she loved him back, his lips were on hers and all that mattered was this man and the love they had for each other. Soon she was up against the wall and she deepened the kiss they shared. Not letting up even for a breath. He inched them both over to the couch in the family room. When he had finally let her lips go, they were both gasping for air. She would let him set the pace this time because he needed it. He needed her to comfort him as he wanted her to.

The pullover T-shirt that she wore quickly came over her head and was thrown to the floor and her bra followed. His hands caressed her mounds he loved so much. Then his head fell into her breasts and he sucked hard on one as he worked his hand over the other. His mouth was now on the other breast and his hands were on the move again. She moaned at the pleasure he was giving her with his tongue. He worked the button and zipper of her jeans. Soon he had pulled them down along with the matching thong she was wearing. She was nude while his clothes were still on. But she could say anything because he turned her mind to mush already from his lovemaking.

She felt his tongue move from her breast he was lavishing. Then he moved to her stomach and lower. He played his tongue around and inside her belly button. She would have never thought her belly button would be one of her many pleasure points. He knew how much she liked it from the moans she was giving him. "You like that, huh, baby?"

Speaking for her was out of the question. All she could do was to shake her head yes. He showered kisses all over her she knew where he was heading. When she felt his breath on the hot spot between her thighs, her hips arched up from the sheer thought of his tongue playing with her clitoris. It excited her and when his mouth finally came on her mound, she gasped and closed her eyes from the pleasure.

He made love to her with his mouth and she could feel she was about to come. Starting where the opening of her tight walls where he circled the entrance but didn't put his tongue in. She moaned out her frustration. He was torturing her with his mouth. He moved upward. She moaned again. He played with her hardened nub. This time she moaned out her pleasure.

He removed his mouth from her and stripped all his clothes off. He was finally bare of clothing and she couldn't wait to have him inside her where he belonged. He lifted one of her legs and rested it on his shoulder while he straddled her other thigh. He pushed inside of her in one smooth thrust and set the tempo. His full-bodied strokes were heavenly. The pleasure was so incredible. She felt as if she would die right there in his arms. He continued to push inside of her, and her walls squeezed at his thick member. Her back was completely off the couch and her release had overtaken her.

"Oh, God, I love you," she yelled at the top of her lungs. Then Juan's release followed soon after, filling her womb with his seed.

"I love you, too." He said, then he was asleep, not caring that he was on the couch stark-naked. Somehow, he found the strength to get them up to their bedroom and laid her in the bed. He lay beside her and she snuggled up against him. With their scent of lovemaking that trailed from the family room, now to the bedroom, he followed her in slumber.

CHAPTER 12

It had been a month, and Carolina was still in her coma and Juan had not gone to visit her in almost a week. Diego was getting bigger every day, and her and Juan's relationship was stronger than ever. She thought about their situation when Sonja heard her cell phone ring. She knew it was her mother. She knew that Ty and Z had talked with her parents about her living arrangement with Juan. She knew they wanted to size him up, but she didn't want to put him through the interrogation of not only her brothers, but her mother and father. "Sonja, it's been a month when are you going to bring him around to meet the family? You know we have a family dinner every Monday night. You should bring him around this Monday."

"I don't know when you all will meet him because there is a lot of stuff going on here." She knew Juan was standing right behind her. And then he did the unthinkable. He placed small kisses on her neck.

"Who's that on the phone?" He lifted his lips from her neck to ask, then went back to his task. She loved her mom, Shana Jacobs, very much, but she knew how to push a person to the edge and speaking of edge, she loved how Juan pushed her over the edge on a regular. They have a routine that they follow, and the only time they disturbed it is when Diego wanted some attention. She thought about the conversation she was having with her mom.

You've been living with him for a month and you can't even have him over for dinner with your family...

"Mom," she said loud enough for Juan to hear her. "It's just not a good time for us to come for a visit."

Before she heard her mother speak Juan grabbed the phone,

introduced himself, and accepted her mother's invitation to dinner on Monday night, then hung up the phone before she could tell her mother anything else.

He passed her cell phone to her. "What was that about? Why did you accept her invite when I just declined?"

"I always hear you talking to your mother and you always decline her invitation to dinner. And I figured that you won't catch a break if you don't just accept. Since you didn't, I did for us. Aren't you happy for us? This way I can ask for your hand."

"Yeah, right, that's what you said two weeks ago. I still haven't found the ring yet." She said while folding her arms over her chest and poking out her bottom lip.

"Monday night I get to meet your family. I'm ready."

"You say that now. But you're not just meeting my brothers and parents. You're meeting aunts, uncles, and cousins. At one point of the night, my father and brothers will take you into his study and grill you silly, just like they've done with every other guy I have brought to the house." She said with a distorted face.

"I will charm them with my wit and intelligence," he said with a charming smile. He pulled her into his arms.

"We have nothing to worry about because we love each other too much to let anything come between us, right?"
She nodded her head yes. He placed a reassuring kiss on her lips.

*   *   *

Monday night they gathered up all the things they would need for Diego and headed to her parent's home. She was trying to tell him about all her family members while leaving everything out about her brothers and parents.

"You know I could care less how your family takes to me," he pulled to a stop in front of her parent's house, grabbed her hand, and looked her square in the eye. "The only one I care about is you and the love that you have for me."

"I'm just nervous. My family means a lot to me and I want them to accept us as a couple."

"I understand where you're coming from," Juan said, glancing at Diego, who had fallen asleep as he drove. *Is our love strong enough to last a lifetime? Would she sacrifice her family for me and Diego?* Juan couldn't help the questions coming to his mind. He did not doubt in his mind that she loved him as he loved her, but could he allow her to choose between the family she's known her entire life?

"Besides, I am a likable guy. I got you to move in with me after just one date, that should say something about my character, right?"

As he parked the car, she turned to him, not believing what he had just said. He had a goofy smile on his face showing he was playing and trying to get her to relax. "You're right, but don't say the last part about us living together. Even though they all know about it, I don't want to broadcast it."

"It's all good, baby. I will get Diego out the back. I don't want to take the whole car seat in. Is that cool with you?"

"Yeah, there are plenty of people here that will want to hold him." She got out of the car and got the baby bag out of the back seat. "I have to warn you my father will probably pull you away from the party, sit you in his study, and question you relentlessly, you up for it?"

She walked around the car, and he gave her a peck on the lips. "I can tell how much this means to you; I'm up for it."

They walked hand in hand towards the front door.

Sonja raised her hand to knock on the door, but it swung open before she got to touch it. "You didn't tell me you were bringing a baby with you. Oh, he is just precious. And so is the man." Juan blushed a little, but only Sonja had

62

seen it. "Come in, come in, everyone's here."

"Hi, Mama," Sonja hugged her mother. Juan could not have mistaken her for anyone else. Sonja's mother was an older version of her. "Juan I'd like for you to meet my mother, Shana Jacobs. Mama, this is Juan Delgado."

"It is nice to finally meet you, Mrs. Jacobs. Sonja has told me so much about you. And this little bundle here is Diego Delgado, my nephew."

"Isn't he just cute? And you can call me Shana." She said as she took hold of the now awake Diego.

"Who is this who has finally made it to my house? Who I haven't seen in more than a month?" A big caramel-skinned man came from around the corner with his arms wide open, coming for a bear hug from his only daughter.

"Hi, Daddy, it hasn't been that long since I've been here. And please be nice." She said, embracing his hug. While he gave Juan a look that said, 'I'll get to you in a minute'. Juan was a proud man, but he knew that this meeting was important to Sonja so he will play nice with her father.

"Daddy this is Juan Delgado and his nephew Diego," she said, pointing to the baby in her mother's hands, "Juan this is my father Desmond Jacobs."
Juan stuck his hand out to shake Mr. Jacobs' hand. But her father didn't take his hand in return. "Be nice, Daddy," Sonja whispered again to her overprotective father. He had been glaring at Juan since he entered the foyer.

"We will talk now." It wasn't a question. But Juan knew he would make a good impression on them in this so-called meeting.

"That's fine with me, sir. Lead the way." He turned to Sonja and took her hands in his. "You look like I've just been sentenced to the death penalty." He kissed her cheek.

"I'll be fine." He followed her father and three other

guys followed in behind him. *Is her family serious? She is a grown woman.*

All of them got to Desmond's home office. A chair was sitting in the middle of the room. He knew he was to sit there and get interrogated.

"Sit down, son. This is Sonja's cousin, Gavin, but he's almost like a brother to her. You know Ty and Z."

"How you guys doing?" They all did the universal head nod.

"What is it you want to ask me?" Juan looked directly at Mr. Desmond.

"Well," he started, "we want to know what you're trying to do with my little girl?"

"With all due respect, sir, she is no longer a little girl. She is a beautiful, caring, and understanding woman. She has already got me wrapped around her finger. Anything that she wants I will try my hardest to provide for her. In the short time that we have known each other, she has become the most important person in my life, even though my sister is in the hospital, barely alive and my nephew may be without a mother before he even got to know her." Juan was babbling but he didn't care. Her father had to either accept him in his daughter's life or leave them alone, and Juan would tell all of them just that. "And if you or your boys here can't..."

"That's enough, son. I think I have heard enough." They looked at each man in the room and in return they each gave him a nod of their head in agreement. Juan didn't know what they were agreeing on. "You were just babbling about your life, you have very strong feelings for Sonja."

"Yes, sir, I am in love with your daughter."

"I already knew that, but it's good to hear that you are saying it aloud. We just don't want to see her hurt."

"I understand. Even though it's not the same, I would treat any man my sister would bring around the same way.

64

"Is that all?"

"Pretty much," Gavin spoke for the first time.

They cleared out, but before anyone got to the door Juan said, "Wait a minute. Sonja said that you would talk to her dates for a long time and interrogate the poor boy. What happened?"

"Are you saying you want more questions?" Ty asked with a look on his face that said that he could think of many questions for him.

"No, I'm cool," Juan said and stood to walk out with them at the end of the line of men. Sonja was waiting for them, sending her siblings a hard look. "Hey, they are just looking out for you and the worst is over. I believe they like me." She turned to him and smiled.

*   *   *

"I can't believe that they only asked you one question." Sonja looked at him in amazement while they were lying in their bed after a two rounds of lovemaking. "Not one man has come to my father's house and gotten asked only one question. I am speechless."

"I just told them what was up. They accepted us as a couple. But it wasn't as horrific as you lead me to believe." Juan got up out of the bed and she moaned her protest. "I'll be right back." He placed a quick kiss on her lips, put on his robe, and walked over to the bathroom. Not that he had to use the throne, but he wanted to make his proposal romantic. He had a dozen red, pink, and white roses, her favorite flower, hidden in the bathroom.

When he came out with the roses in his hand, she thought nothing of it. He had always brought her flowers in the middle of the day or night. It was sweet. It also gave him extra points.

"These are for you."

"Thank You," she exclaimed, blushing. She had no idea what he was doing, even though he was getting down on one knee.

"Even though we have known each other for a short month and in some ways, I feel as if I've known you all my life. And every time I wake up with you beside me, I just can't imagine you not in my life."

His phone started ringing. He looked as if he would ignore it, but she said, "It could be some wonderful news about your sister." He gave a scoff of disbelief and answered the phone.

"This is Dr. Kelly and your sister is fully awake. Her vitals are all stable. When you get here, she will be ready to see you and Diego."

"Thank you, doctor. We will be there as soon as possible." He looked up at Sonja and his eyes filled with tears. She didn't know if those were happy or sad tears, but she brought his head into her chest and he wept because he knew his sister would be fine.

"Baby, she will be fine. The doctor said that she has been up for about five hours. But Dr. Kelly didn't want to call us until they knew for sure she would be okay. And she will be okay." He said with a big, bright smile on his face. He could not be any happier. Nope, that wasn't true if they had called after Sonja had said yes to his proposal, then he would be a man on top of the world.

*   *   *

At the hospital, they could see Carolina right away. Sonja told them she would get some coffee, and she did, but she also went to the waiting room so he and his sister would get some privacy.

She stayed in the waiting room for about half an hour, thinking about her life. She knew she wanted to be with

Juan and have his children. She also knew Juan was in the middle of proposing to her, and she would accept. If only he would drop to one knee again. She wouldn't even let him get the question out before she said yes.

CHAPTER 13

She returned to the hospital room. And found Carolina holding her child and getting to know Diego and Juan in front of the door on bended knee. "My first proposal was interrupted," he looked at his sister and she mouthed the words 'sorry'. "But this time it won't be. So, will you take me as your…"

"Yes. I will be your wife." She said before he could finish. "I told myself that I would say yes to you before you even finish the question or before any interruptions." They all laughed.

Juan stood up and gave her a deep tongue wrestling kiss.

"Save it for the wedding night," his sister said. But they stayed locked in each other's arms for just a few more minutes.

*   *   *

"When are you going to tell your parents?" Juan asked as they were driving home from the hospital holding his fiancé's hand.

"I would call them up tonight, but it's way too late for that. I will call them first thing in the morning. I figured you would wait to ask because we were there seeing your sister. She is genuinely nice. I know Diego will be happy to finally be with his mother." She looked back at Diego, who was now sleeping in his car seat.

"You and Carolina hit it off nicely. I am thrilled that my sister and my future wife are getting along." He glanced at her as he was pulling up in the driveway.

"So," he put the car in park and looked her in the eyes, "what do you think about kids?"

The look in his green eyes said he wanted a house full of

children. "I want a quick wedding within the next six months." She said with no hesitation. "I want to fill our house with children that have the best of you and the best of me. We can start tonight."

Once Juan heard that, he was quickly out of the car with Diego and got around to her car door to open it. They rushed into the house. Sonja was allowing him to make love to her flesh to flesh. The last time was a slip-up, them being caught up in the magic. She felt good with a condom, but now he will feel the sensational pleasure of going bare. He couldn't have gotten Diego ready for bed and in his crib fast enough.

Sonja knew that Juan was getting Diego ready for bed and she wanted to make their lovemaking extra special tonight. She had on a champagne-colored teddy and lit candles all around the room. She lit the last candle and Juan stepped into the room and saw the mood she was creating.

"You didn't have to set the mood. Looking at you is enough to get me in the mood."

"Why don't you come over here and you can show me what kind of mood you're in."

And he did. His mouth immediately went straight for her. His hands were on her curve of her butt, pushing her pelvis to his. Trying to get her closer, but not close enough.

She suddenly felt her legs lifted from underneath her and Juan picked her up and walked her to the bed. But their mouths locked in the kiss they haven't ended yet.

Sonja was then airborne, and Juan was right behind her. They were both in the air, about to land right on the bed.

They both laughed, "I did not expect for you to throw me into bed like that." He wrapped her up in his arms and brought his head down to the tops of her breasts. And slowly he pulled the straps down her arms. The only thing on his mind was making love to the woman that he loved so much that he would give her his name and his child.

The next thing she knew, her teddy was off. Juan's hands were everywhere. Burning every inch of her skin and making her want more. He was making her lose herself in his exploration of her body like he had done many times over.

They were laying right next to each other with his chest to her breast. Sonja took the lovemaking into her own hands. She pushed Juan to his back, straddled his thighs, and ripped his clothes off, not worrying where they landed on the floor. And soon they were both naked and ready for each other.

Juan still letting Sonja have her time, loved the way her soft hands felt on his hard body. She reached to his neck and massaged down to his hips, but it felt like she was touching down to his toes. He could feel her everywhere and he loved that feeling.

He brought her face down to his for a long and sensual kiss. He rolled her onto her back, "When we make love tonight you will feel all of me and I will feel all of you. And when my seed spills into your body, it will be to create a love child."

He quickly kissed her, giving her no time to respond to him. Whatever she was about to say halted when Juan slid his finger inside of her, making sure she was ready for him as he was ready for her. He stroked and stroked his finger inside her. She moaned. He added a finger. She moaned louder and louder and louder.

Juan released his fingers from her tight grip and pushed all of his hard manhood inside her, and she screamed in pleasure. He waited a minute, just being in her womanly channel felt so good, then he moved slowly, making her gasp for air. He could tell how much she was enjoying it. The pleasure intensified tenfold.

Juan pumped faster and harder into her, and as he did, she

screamed, yelped, and noises were getting louder and stronger. He felt her walls getting tighter and knew she was about to explode in the best orgasm of her adult life.

Her body withered beneath him, and he held her close. Her orgasm hit her like a ton of bricks. The orgasm set him off to come. His warm seed spread through her womb and that thought alone set off another orgasm. He gently pulled himself out of her and went to go get a cloth to clean her, then himself.

Afterward, they lay in the sweet smell of their lovemaking. The last thought in Juan's head was that he could hold Sonja like this for the rest of their lives together.

*   *   *

Sonja went to her parents' home first thing in the morning to find only her mother, but she just could not wait to tell them together.

"Are you serious?" Sonja's mother asked in excitement.

"But you have only known each other for a couple of months." She paused, and Sonja was a little afraid of what she would say next. "But I know from personal experience that love knows no time." She said with a big smile, remembering how long it took her to fall in love with her husband. "I'm so happy for you."

"Why?" Her father walked in right as her mother was hugging her with her blessing.

"I'm getting married; Daddy, Juan and I are engaged," Sonja said, thinking about her father walking her down the aisle to her future husband.

"Oh, really."

They thought he would continue, but he didn't finish his thought.

"Is that all you have to say 'oh, really'. I just told you I

71

found Juan who will love me and be beside me for the rest of my life and that's all you have to say?" He had two angry females in his face at this point.

"Well, he didn't go through the right channels."

"What right channels?" Sonja was getting mad quickly.

"Me. Someone has asked for your hand in marriage already. And I gave him my blessing." He said with a big smile like Sonja and his wife would be happy he said so.

"Daddy, what are you talking about? Who asked to marry me?"

"Mathis, he will be here in a few. It was supposed to be a surprise." Desmond said as if he was satisfied with the decision he made for her life.

"What did you just say?" She paused to see if he would retract what he said. "What gives you the right to decide who will be my husband? Do you see how angry I am with you right now? I could just…"

"I will stop you right there," her father said, "I am still your father and I know who would be best for you."

"If you think it is Mathis, then you do not know me very well." Sonja turned to her mother, "I'm leaving, Mama," she hugged her and mugged her father out the door.

When she opened the door, Mathis was walking up to the door, and so was Juan. She knew things would go from bad to worse in two-point two seconds. Mathis saw that Sonja was looking past him and towards someone behind him. He turned to see who was there. His face completely changed knowing what would come next.

Juan saw the flowers in Mathis's hands and became furious. Sonja had never seen him so upset. "I thought I told you to stay away from Sonja."

"You're too late, Juan," Mathis said his name with malice and triumph in his tone, "I will finally have Sonja in my life forever as my wife. Her father and I arranged it."

Juan looked at Sonja, knowing that there had to be lies spilling out of her ex-boyfriend's mouth. He had to be lying because she had just accepted his proposal last night.

"Juan," he heard his name on her lips, "he is not lying." Juan immediately turned around and headed to his car. Sonja caught up with him before he could get into the car and drive away. She told him all her father had told her about Mathis going behind her back and asking to marry her and her father giving Mathis his blessing.

At this point, Juan saw red like never before. Mathis had the fight of his life coming for him. Juan looked like a lion coming to protect his lioness. Before Mathis knew it, he had a fist full of Juan's anger coming toward his face. Juan got in one good hit and Mathis fell to the hard cement.

Sonja's parents were outside in a flash and Juan was ready to take his anger out on Desmond, Sonja's father. "Out of respect for Sonja and her lovely mother," he gave Shana a polite nod of the head and she nodded back understanding his position, then looked back at Desmond, "I will talk to you later." Juan walked away and grabbed Sonja's hand as they got into the car and drove off.

*   *   *

"How could he have put you in that situation?" That was the only question Juan could ask out loud. Sonja had nothing to say to excuse her father's behavior. She just sat in the car waiting to get back to the house. The car ride was as slow as ever and she just wanted to get somewhere and cry long and hard at how her father betrayed her.

When they finally got to the house Sonja didn't wait for Juan to get her door, she flew out so fast he barely had time to cut the engine off. She darted out of the car and used her key to get into the house. Juan couldn't even blame her. He

73

knew how upset she was from her silence. He would just wait a couple of minutes to let her have some time alone. Then he would hold her in a tight embrace that no one could ever penetrate.

Minutes later, he walked into their bedroom to find her curled up in a ball. He came over in front of her, brushed the tears from her eyes, picked her up, and set her on his lap. She was straddling him with her face buried into his chest. He held her like that for what seemed to be forever. He kissed the top of her head and whispered loud enough for her to hear, "I will never let no one hurt you like that again and if someone gets to you, I will always be here to hold you." He kissed her on her head again.

CHAPTER 14

Sonja was so angry with her father, she needed Juan right now in the worst way. And he was happy to oblige. He let her take control of their lovemaking. She laid him down on the bed with his feet still dangling off the edge of the bed. She straddled his thighs, then wiped her face of excess tears and went down to work. Starting at the top of his head and giving him the same loving forehead kiss, he gave her. She kissed each of his cheeks, giving just a little tongue, then she went to his nose. His lips were just waiting to connect with hers. He drank her. But still she was in control. She explored his mouth and in return; he did the same. He will always love kissing her. He could kiss her the entire night and would be satisfied and would want to keep kissing her every day. She moved her lips from his as he moaned a protest while stealing just one more kiss and a small kiss on his chin.

Still clothed at this point, they started shedding clothes. First, it was his shirt where she was slowly, god awfully slow-moving down his chest, eating at his skin and thoroughly tonguing his flat nipples. She lightly kissed the dusted hair of his happy trail, which she could tell it thrilled him to have her on top this time.

Slowly, she unbutton his pants and pull the zipper down. Finally, she got his pants and boxers off, and now she was about to blow his mind. She gave him a wicked smile and ever so gently kissed the tip of his shaft, and just for that, he moaned because he knew what was coming next.

Sonja put the head of his cock inside her mouth and teased it. She wrapped her tongue around the large head and she knew Juan loved all the attention she was giving him. She slowly descended to his engorged shaft. She wanted all of

75

him inside her mouth, but he was too big. She squeezed her mouth tighter around him and he gave a small involuntary moan. She came up for air and went down once again. She stroked his shaft with one hand, while the other played with his sensitive to the touch sacks, and her mouth doing amazing things up and down his shaft.

When Juan could not take any more teasing from her mouth, he picked her up as if she was nothing and they traded places. He was now between her legs. She could feel his breath on her thighs. "My turn," was all he said. She was so ready for him. He started licking up her inner thigh, and after going up one he went back down to the other thigh and gave them equal attention. He kissed her on top of her clit. It made her arch immediately. He pulled and tugged at it. And it was driving her crazy. He then gave a full tongue, licking from her opening to the tip. She moaned. He did it again. She continued to moan as he continued. His tongue got faster and faster, working his tongue inside her womanly channel. She opened her eyes and saw his head going to work on her, and she moaned even louder. Then he pushed two fingers inside her and that was all she needed. She came harder than ever before.

Juan gave her no time to recover and instantly thrust his angry shaft inside her. This was not one of those slow lovemaking sessions. This was sex, even though they are deeply in love. He used long, full-bodied strokes. She was moaning, just begging for another orgasm like she just had. His strokes were getting faster and harder. He was taking her to the highest of heights. And somehow, he was there with her. He could feel her walls squeezing him tighter and tighter and knew they were about to come together. His seed spilled into her and triggered her second orgasm.

When he pulled out, he was still hard, not that she didn't satisfy him, but he wanted more of her. Sonja finally caught

76

a deep breath after that amazing orgasm they shared. She sat up and saw his still inflated penis. He was ready for round two and so was she.

Sonja caught him off guard and pushed him to the bed, climbed on top of him and slid down his shaft one more time. She used her womanly muscles to squeeze him before she even moved for the first stroke. "You like teasing me, don't you?"

All she could do was nod her head yes and gave him a wicked smile. She moved to give him the first stroke, which was long and easy. She went all the way to the tip and slammed down to his sack. She did it repeatedly, while Juan played with her bouncing breasts that were already in his face. She grinded into him, getting all of him inside of her, and he held on to her hips. Their sexual rhythm had started.

He raised his upper body and came up for a deep kiss. While she was still grinding on him, his hand was on her round bottom pushing her that much closer to him. Sonja threw her head back but fell on her back. Juan was there to change their position. Now her legs were around his hips and he was giving his famous, good loving, full-bodied thrust into her and she was a goner. Once again, he took her to the heights, and they were there together. She came like a chain reaction. He spilled his seed inside her once more, hoping to have created a child.

They lay for long minutes and his semi-erection still inside her. He found the strength to lay them upright, where the pillows were ready for their heads, and cover them with the throw blanket at the foot of the bed.

They went to sleep, sweat coating their bodies in each other's arms.

                    *   *   *

Saturday mornings were always a delight for Sonja, even though her father did what he did. But waking in the afterglow of their lovemaking made her feel that much better. When Sonja awoke instead of finding Juan's warm body, she found a note attached to his pillow. It reads "Sweetheart, I had to leave to get Diego and Carolina together to go home." He signed it love J.

Juan's sister, Carolina, was showing nothing but improvements over the last couple of days and the doctor has given her the go-ahead to go home and be with her son. It was great news, and she wanted to be there to share it with Juan's family.

Sonja dressed and ready for them to come home to gather up the last of Diego's things. It will be the first time she will have seen Carolina out of a hospital gown. She was sitting in the living room sipping on her coffee when the doorbell rang. She jumped up knowing who was at the door and she stopped right in her tracks when she saw her parents standing there. Her face completely changed from excitement to mocking disdain. "Hello, Mama, how are you," then looked directly into her father's eyes, "You should have called first."

They waited to be invited in. She did not offer. Her mother offered for her. "We knew that if we called you would have made sure you weren't here. So, we just dropped by." There was a pregnant pause. "Are you going to make us stand out here for the entire conversation or can we come in?"

"Fine." She turned on her heels, knowing that they would follow her. Before she could go in on her father, he spoke.

"I'm sorry, Pudding." He used her childhood nickname

78

only he used. He used it often when she was mad at him and he had to apologize. All she could do was shake her head.

"My nickname will not make everything better this time, Daddy. You told a man that he could marry me when I haven't even spoken to him in the last month in a half. You know the last time I saw him, he was sitting on my couch happy as ever. After we broke up, he duplicated my front door key. If Juan weren't there, I don't know what would have happened."

"Why didn't you tell us all of this?" Her father asked.

"How can I protect you if I don't know the whole story?"

"You didn't need to know it all. You just needed to know that Mathis and I were not together as a couple any longer and left it at that."

Desmond could do nothing but put his head down in shame. "I can do nothing else but apologize for my behavior." He looked her in the eye with a playful glee.

"We would also like to throw you an engagement party. That way I can start on better ground with Juan."

Sonja could not believe her ears. *An engagement party,* Juan and Sonja were already planning to have one, but to pay the cost for the wedding and an engagement party would have been a lot. They'd plan to have them about six months apart, but with them paying for the engagement party, they could get married sooner. "We appreciate all that you have offered." They all turned around to find Juan standing there. "Sir, Ma'am, could I steal Sonja away for just a minute?" He grabbed her hand and walked out of the room before they could answer his question.

Once in the kitchen, the first thing he did was wrap her in his warmth and kiss her like he should have this morning.

"Good morning." He said with a bright smile. "I know you would not turn down your parent's invitation to pay for

79

the engagement party."

"No, I wasn't, but I wanted to talk it over with you first. If they pay for the party, we can get married sooner than we planned."

"Well, let's talk it over since they are your parents. Your father messed up big time, but we should forgive him. Parents make mistakes all the time, and it probably won't be the last." She still didn't look all the way convinced. "When we become parents, don't you want our little girl to forgive me after I run one of her boyfriends off?" That put a smile on her face. She realized that her cold shoulder was just making her father miserable.

"So, we agree that we should take them up on paying for the engagement party?" He nodded his head in agreement. They returned to the living room to tell her parents the good news. It overjoyed them they could help with their only daughter's wedding. They gave rounds of hugs among the men. Soon Shana pulled her daughter aside and started asking her all kinds of questions about the wedding and the color scheme. Sonja had to stop her mother and told her they would have lunch and talk through all the preparations.

CHAPTER 15

They prepared everything for their engagement party. They gathered all of their family and friends to celebrate the news of their engagement. And they were all waiting for the grand entrance of Sonja, the bride-to-be, especially Juan.

He was already at the engagement party waiting for his soon-to-be-wife. He was ecstatic. He knew that in another short month they would make it all official. And he couldn't contain his smile.

"So, Juan, do you have any other plans for the company?" John, one of the chief executive officers, asked him.

"Lay off the man," Shawn came riding in to save the groom and best friend. "We can talk about business when he gets back from his honeymoon," Shawn said as he was turning Juan in another direction. "Let me buy you a drink."

"It's an open bar, but okay," Juan said, feeling a little nervous knowing that the ten o'clock hour was about to strike. Sonja was to enter at exactly ten-thirty. He knew her dress was going to be red wine since the colors for the wedding was red wine and black. Even though she would not allow him to see either dress for the ceremony or the engagement party, he knew in whatever she wore it would be the most beautiful thing to see. But more than anything he would much rather have her naked and beneath him or above him.

He was getting lost in his world of Sonja while Shawn had been talking the entire time. He had to catch up on the conversation so he would not look so stupid when the topic came around to him.

*   *   *

Who do they think they are? Mathis questioned himself. *They have no idea who they are dealing with. I know all about the proposal, the engagement, and the wedding that was supposed to be for them. How could she not choose me?* It was all good because he knew what limo escort services they used. He would do something about them being together and make it like it was supposed to be.

Mathis was waiting in front of Juan's house, just waiting for the limo to come along so he could put his plan into action. There was his limo that would pick up his favorite girl. But she will get a surprise of a lifetime. He walked up to the limo. The driver was sitting there texting one of his contacts. Mathis could tell from the light; he saw on the driver's phone. *I guess he wasn't expecting to have a gun shoved in his face and hit over the head tonight.* He said with a giggle as if the kidnapping was a normal occurrence for him.

Mathis yanked the door open and startled the limo driver. Mathis quietly raised the gun up to the temple of his head. He told him to get out of the driver's seat; he asked for the keys and walked him to the bushes where he was hiding and hit him over the head with the wine bottle that he was nursing. Mathis had no intention to kill the driver, just knock him out for a while.

Mathis went back to the limo and opened the back passenger's door and was on his way to the driver's side. *A pleasant evening it will be.* Mathis thought to himself with a wicked smile.

*   *   *

Sonja looked at herself in the mirror. She was on her way to the man of her dreams. It was exactly ten o'clock and her mother and father were already in their limousine and on the way to the hotel. Her limo driver was waiting for her to leave the house and take her to Juan.

She double-checked to make sure she had her purse, an extra pair of shoes, and her overnight bag because she and Juan planned to stay at the hotel to do a little celebrating themselves. Sonja was ready, but before she left out, she made sure she locked all the doors. Sonja was ready to get the party started. The door was already open. The driver was sitting in the front, ready to go. She jumped into her seat and closed the door quickly. The driver already knew where he was to take her, so no words were exchanged.

A while later as she saw they were about to get onto the highway, she was about to question the driver's directions, eager to get to Juan. But before she could, he spoke. "Did you think you and your precious little boyfriend were getting rid of me that fast?" Then everything went black.

*　　*　　*

It was getting late, and Juan was getting nervous.

Juan knew Sonja should walk into the ballroom at ten-thirty. It was almost eleven-fifteen. Shawn, his best man, was keeping him company and trying to occupy his mind. But all Juan wanted to see right now was Sonja, who was supposed to be there at ten-thirty sharp.

The impatient groom-to-be could not wait any longer. He would go get his bride. As he was walking out, a man in black dress pants can through the door.

He was out of breath. "I'm looking for Juan Delgado. I need to speak to him," the man said.

"I'm Juan Delgado." Juan saw he was wearing the same logo on his pants as the driver for Sonja's parents. "Aren't you the driver for my fiancée? Is she here?" Juan asked with a smile on his face and then looked back at the driver.

"No, something isn't right. What happened to Sonja?"

The driver told him what happened and what the guy looked like who beat him over the head with a wine bottle. Juan was thinking this smelled of Mathis doing before the driver told him what he looked like.

Juan was seeing red and was ready to just about kill Mathis for even touching the woman that belonged to him. He thanked the driver for coming all this way to inform him of what had happened and put him in a cab. Juan paid the toll to get him home safely.

Juan immediately gathered Sonja's father, brothers, and Shawn together. The conference room was very silent until Juan spoke.

"Mathis has lost his mind and taken Sonja." All the men in the room could tell now was not the time to play with Juan because the veins were popping out of his neck and forehead. "He knocked the driver out who was supposed to bring Sonja to our engagement party and drove her God knows where. And I need your help to find her." He was pleading with the other men. That is when Sonja's father saw the love that he had for his daughter. "I need her in my life and if anything happens to her when she is with him, I will kill him." All the men nodded their heads in agreement. "Now, does anyone know where he might have taken her? A remote place where there is a lot of space somewhere where they won't be seen?"

Her father spoke up, "You know my very accomplished nephew owns and works at the Hidden Investigative Firm." He looked right at Gavin. He had a wicked, he-is-not-getting-far smile on his face.

CHAPTER 16

Less than an hour later, Gavin walked back into the room. All the men were dressed in jeans and T-shirts, clothing that you could beat someone down in. "That man is an actual idiot. He used his credit card to check out a cabin just about a 30-minute drive from here." He passed them all directions and Juan was the first out of the door. He knew they would come up with something to get there themselves, but it was long overdue for him to see Sonja. Gavin had already gotten which cabin number they were in, and the information was on the map. Juan was on his way to kill.

Meanwhile, Gavin called the police, and they piled into two cars and started on their way to be a witness to plead temporary insanity for Juan.

*   *   *

Sonja knew she was in trouble when she was in the limo. She just had a feeling that something would go wrong, but she shook it off. All she wanted to think about was Juan and how he made her feel whenever they were around each other. Now she was in a random place and tied to a chair so she couldn't move anywhere.

When she finally came to her senses Mathis was sitting across from her at a table that looked to be set for a romantic evening.

"Well, I didn't think I knocked you out that hard, sweetheart. You've been out for a little under two hours."

"How dare you call me that after you have stolen me from the man that I love on the night that we would announce our love to the world?" Mathis got up so fast, turned the table over, and was in her face in a matter of seconds. The table set for two was now on the floor in a pile of utensils and plates.

"It should be with me!" He shouted into her face, "You should marry me and love me. But you didn't. You betrayed my love and now you will be punished." Before Sonja knew the whole side of her face was pounding from the slap that was just delivered from Mathis' hand.

Regardless of the slap she just received, it did not stop her from giving her piece. "If I would have known you would turn out this crazy, I would not have entertained you for even a year and a half." She could tell her words were getting to him as he froze stiff just listening to what she had to say.

"I was never looking to get into a serious relationship with you." She was getting the rope that he tied her hands together loose. "I always told you you were just there. You were fun. But now I have a man that can keep me on my toes and give me what I need and not be crazy like you are acting right now." Just a little more and she would be free.

"Let me tell you, I feel sorry for you when Juan gets his hands on you and after him, you must deal with my brothers, then my father," Finally the rope was free from her hands and she was just about to take him down, "But right now you will have to deal with me."

Sonja's right hand came full force with an uppercut to his chin. She hit him so hard she heard his teeth chatter. He wasn't expecting her to hit him, and he dropped the gun he was carrying. It stunned Mathis. He did not know that she had recently taken some self-defense and boxing classes at a nearby center.

Immediately after the first blow, she kicked him right between his legs, a direct hit. He doubled over. Just then the front door came crashing down. It was Juan coming to save her. They locked eyes, and he saw the faint red handprint on the side of her beautiful face. He saw red once again. And he directed all his anger at the man who was already on the floor holding on to his balls.

Juan could not think, all he knew was he was beating on Mathis face. After a good while, he let up on his face and tears begin streaming down. Mathis face was all bloody, and Juan's knuckles were bruised and bloodied. Without even thinking, Juan turned and picked Sonja into his arms and headed for the door where he saw the police had finally made it. He was about six feet from the front door, still carrying her. Then he heard a loud pop and felt a sharp pain in his shoulder.

*   *   *

Juan didn't remember what happened after he heard the loud pop because everything went black. The next day he woke up in a hospital bed where Sonja was right beside him, holding his hand. He squeezed her hand and she realized that he was up.

It relieved Sonja he was awake and could speak. But the first thing he wanted to do was give her a long kiss that he had wanted to give her at the night of their engagement party. "I am so happy that you are okay." She said with a trembling voice and a single tear fell from her eye.

"Hey now," Juan said reassuringly, "you aren't getting rid of me that soon. We have a lifetime to live out together." He wiped her tear from her face. "Baby, what happened?" Sonja told him that even though he beat his face enough for two lifetimes, he could still get off one shot with his eyesight and the bullet hit him in the shoulder blade but it didn't pierce the bone and the bullet exited his shoulder. The police took Mathis away. They charged him with a kidnapping and attempted murder.

Since the bullet went in and out of Juan's shoulder. They cleared him to leave the hospital after a week to be sure that there were no internal injuries. There was no infection. He had to wear a sling for a month before they cleared him.

"I do not wear a sling on my wedding day," Juan proclaimed. He looked at Sonja, "Coming to you after that psycho took you from me. I would do it all again. I will fully recover before we walk down the aisle. And I love you."

Then he gave her a kiss, knowing that she needed that reassurance.

EPILOGUE

2 Months Later

Juan was cleared to go on without the need of a sling. They would finally get married. Juan thought, as he paced the entrance of where he was to walk with the minister. Every night since the shooting, he had not left her side. It took her brothers and cousin to promise they would not leave her side until her father was walking her to me. An image he will never forget.

"Daddy tell them to leave me alone for a minute! It is my day and I want to have some peace, but I cannot have that with them hovering around me," Sonja said in a huff.

"Usually, I would give you your space, but they are under strict orders from your soon-to-be." Her father said.
Sonja gave her sweetest look and puppy dog eyes. He looked at the boys and they started clearing out.

"You've got twenty minutes, Dad." Z stated while shutting the door.

"All right, Pudding, are you ready to get married?"
Sonja could not believe it was finally time. She jumped up, checked her makeup, and went to the door. Before she knew it, she was in front of Juan with her father giving her away.

"You may now kiss your bride." The preacher proclaimed.
Juan, with a big smile on his face, lifted her veil happily, "Together forever, you came to me right on time." He whispered close to her lips before taking them to seal their future forever.

ABOUT THE AUTHOR

Lauren Stansberry is a mother of two beautiful children. She is originally from Indianapolis, IN, home grown. She loves black love and a romantic down to the bone. And she loves to go out dancing. She has been dancing for about ten years now, off and on. She loves to travel and visit family out of town. Her biggest value is family and friends.

www.ingramcontent.com/pod-product-compliance
Lightning Source LLC
Chambersburg PA
CBHW060429260626
47161CB00005B/1850